THE JAPANESE FAIRY BOOK

Prince Yamato Take bade his wife help him
to attire himself like a woman.

The
Japanese Fairy Book

COMPILED BY

YEI THEODORA OZAKI

CHARLES E. TUTTLE COMPANY
Rutland, Vermont & Tokyo, Japan

Published by the Charles E. Tuttle Company, Inc.
of Rutland, Vermont & Tokyo, Japan
with editorial offices at
Suido 1-chome, 2–6, Bunkyo-ku, Tokyo, Japan

Library of Congress Catalog Card No. 70–109415
International Standard Book No. 0–8048–0885–6

First Tuttle edition, 1970
Twenty-third printing, 1989

PRINTED IN JAPAN

TABLE OF CONTENTS

———

Table of Contents

PUBLISHER'S FOREWORD

———

FAIRY tales never go out of style; they are the stuff of dreams and life and imagination, immortalized in the human spirit.

These beautiful legends and tales of old Japan were written for the children of the West, and have been translated from the modern version by Sadanami Sanjin. They are not literal translations, although the Japanese story and all quaint Japanese expressions have been faithfully preserved. In a few instances, to enhance interest and enjoyment, the compiler has used incidents from other versions.

The quaint Japanese expressions have been superbly matched by the quaint but evocative and humanly stirring illustrations by Kakuzo Fujiyama, an artist who lived in Tokyo. There are 66 pictures for the 22 tales, an average of three for each tale.

The tales are about commoners and kings; castles and fairylands; good old folks and bad old folks; princesses and warriors; animals, birds, the sky and sea, and the illimitable realms of the imagination.

The stories are the old favorites, such as "Momotaro, or the Story of the Son of a Peach," and "The Story of Urashima Taro, the Fisher Lad"—and many of the lesser known ones such as "The Stones of Five Colours and the Empress Jokwa."

All will have wide appeal to children whose minds and imaginations transcend racial barriers. The "twain shall meet" through the medium of these delightful magic carpets. This book was originally published by Archibold Constable & Co., Ltd., Westminster.

PREFACE

THIS collection of Japanese fairy tales is the outcome of a suggestion made to me indirectly through a friend by Mr. Andrew Lang. They have been translated from the modern version written by Sadanami Sanjin. These stories are not literal translations, and though the Japanese story and all quaint Japanese expressions have been faithfully preserved, they have been told more with the view to interest young readers of the West than the technical student of folk-lore.

Grateful acknowledgment is due to Mr. Y. Yasuoka, Miss Fusa Okamoto, my brother Nobumori Ozaki, Dr. Yoshihiro Takaki, and Miss Kameko Yamao, who have helped me with translations.

The story which I have named "The Story of the Man who did not Wish to Die" is taken from a little book written a hundred years ago by one Shinsui Tamenaga. It is named *Chosei Furo*, or "Longevity." "The Bamboo-cutter and the Moon-child" is taken from the classic "Taketari Monogatari," and is *not* classed by the Japanese among their fairy tales, though it really belongs to this class of literature.

The pictures were drawn by Mr. Kakuzo Fujiyama, a Tokio artist.

In telling these stories in English I have followed my fancy in adding such touches of local colour or description as they seemed to need or as pleased me, and in one or two instances I have gathered in an incident from another version. At all times, among my friends, both young and old, English or American, I have always found eager listeners to the beautiful legends and fairy tales of Japan, and in telling them I have also found that they were still unknown to the vast majority, and this has encouraged me to write them for the children of the West.

Y. T. O.

LIST OF ILLUSTRATIONS

———

List of Illustrations

JAPANESE FAIRY BOOK.

MY LORD BAG OF RICE.

Long, long ago there lived in Japan a brave warrior known to all as Tawara Toda, or " My Lord Bag of Rice." His true name was Fujiwara Hidesato, and there is a very interesting story of how he came to change his name.

One day he sallied forth in search of adventures, for he had the nature of a warrior and could not bear to be idle. So he buckled on his two swords, took his huge bow, much taller than himself, in his hand, and slinging his quiver on his back started out. He had not gone far when he came to the bridge of Seta-no-Karashi spanning one end of the beautiful Lake Biwa. No sooner had he set foot on the bridge than he saw lying right across his path a huge serpent-dragon. Its body was so big that it looked like the trunk of a large pine tree and it took up the whole width of the bridge. One of its huge claws rested on the parapet of one side of the bridge, while its tail lay right against the other. The monster seemed to be asleep, and as it breathed, fire and smoke came out of its nostrils.

At first Hidesato could not help feeling alarmed at the sight of this horrible reptile lying in his path, for he must either

turn back or walk right over its body. He was a brave man,
however, and putting aside all fear went forward dauntlessly.
Crunch, crunch! he stepped now on the dragon's body, now
between its coils, and without even one glance backward he
went on his way.

He had only gone a few steps when he heard someone
calling him from behind. On turning back he was much surprised to see that the monster dragon had entirely disappeared
and in its place was a strange-looking man, who was bowing
most ceremoniously to the ground. His red hair streamed over
his shoulders and was surmounted by a crown in the shape of
a dragon's head, and his sea-green dress was patterned with
shells. Hidesato knew at once that this was no ordinary
mortal and he wondered much at the strange occurrence.
Where had the dragon gone in such a short space of time?
Or had it transformed itself into this man, and what did the
whole thing mean? While these thoughts passed through his
mind he had come up to the man on the bridge and now
addressed him:

" Was it you that called me just now?"

" Yes, it was I," answered the man; " I have an earnest
request to make to you. Do you think you can grant it to
me?"

" If it is in my power to do so I will," answered Hidesato,
" but first tell me who you are?"

" I am the Dragon King of the Lake, and my home is in
these waters just under this bridge."

" And what is it you have to ask of me?" said Hidesato.

" I want you to kill my mortal enemy the centipede, who

lives on the mountain beyond," and the Dragon King pointed to a high peak on the opposite shore of the lake.

Putting aside all Fear, he went forward Dauntlessly.

" I have lived now for many years in this lake and I have a large family of children and grandchildren. For some time past we have lived in terror, for a monster centipede has discovered our home, and night after night it comes and carries off one of my family. I am powerless to save them. If it goes on much longer like this, not only shall I lose all my children, but I myself must fall a victim to the monster. I am, therefore, very unhappy, and in my extremity I determined to ask the help of a human being. For many days with this intention I have waited on the bridge in the shape of the horrible serpent-dragon that you saw, in the hope that some strong brave man would come along. But all who came this way, as soon as they saw me were terrified and ran away as fast as they could. You are the first man I have found able to look at me without fear, so I knew at once that you were a man of great courage. I beg you to have pity upon me. Will you not help me and kill my enemy the centipede?"

Hidesato felt very sorry for the Dragon King on hearing his story, and readily promised to do what he could to help him. The warrior asked where the centipede lived, so that he might attack the creature at once. The Dragon King replied that its home was on the mountain Mikami, but that as it came every night at a certain hour to the palace of the lake, it would be better to wait till then. So Hidesato was conducted to the palace of the Dragon King, under the bridge. Strange to say, as he followed his host downwards the waters parted to let them pass, and his clothes did not even feel damp as he passed through the flood. Never had Hidesato seen anything so beautiful as this palace built of white marble beneath the lake. He had often heard of the Sea King's Palace at the bottom of the sea, where all the servants and retainers were salt-water fishes, but here was a magnificent building in the heart of

Lake Biwa.   The dainty goldfishes, red carp, and silvery trout, waited upon the Dragon King and his guest.

Hidesato was astonished at the feast that was spread for him.   The dishes were crystallised lotus leaves and flowers, and the chopsticks were of the rarest ebony.   As soon as they sat down, the sliding doors opened and ten lovely goldfish dancers came out, and behind them followed ten red-carp musicians with the koto and the samisen.   Thus the hours flew by till midnight, and the beautiful music and dancing had banished all thoughts of the centipede.   The Dragon King was about to pledge the warrior in a fresh cup of wine when the palace was suddenly shaken by a tramp, tramp! as if a mighty army had begun to march not far away.

Hidesato and his host both rose to their feet and rushed to the balcony, and the warrior saw on the opposite mountain two great balls of glowing fire coming nearer and nearer. The Dragon King stood by the warrior's side trembling with fear.

" The centipede ! The centipede ! Those two balls of fire are its eyes.   It is coming for its prey !   Now is the time to kill it."

Hidesato looked where his host pointed, and, in the dim light of the starlit evening, behind the two balls of fire he saw the long body of an enormous centipede winding round the mountains, and the light in its hundred feet glowed like so many distant lanterns moving slowly towards the shore.

Hidesato showed not the least sign of fear.   He tried to calm the Dragon King.

" Don't be afraid.   I shall surely kill the centipede.   Just bring me my bow and arrows."

Hidesato took another Arrow.

The Dragon King did as he was bid, and the warrior noticed that he had only three arrows left in his quiver. He took the bow, and fitting an arrow to the notch, took careful aim and let fly.

The arrow hit the centipede right in the middle of its head, but instead of penetrating, it glanced off harmless and fell to the ground.

Nothing daunted, Hidesato took another arrow, fitted it to the notch of the bow and let fly. Again the arrow hit the mark, it struck the centipede right in the middle of its head, only to glance off and fall to the ground. The centipede was invulnerable to weapons ! When the Dragon King saw that even this brave warrior's arrows were powerless to kill the centipede, he lost heart and began to tremble with fear.

The warrior saw that he had now only one arrow left in his quiver, and if this one failed he could not kill the centipede. He looked across the waters. The huge reptile had wound its horrid body seven times round the mountain and would soon come down to the lake. Nearer and nearer gleamed the fireballs of eyes, and the light of its hundred feet began to throw reflections in the still waters of the lake.

Then suddenly the warrior remembered that he had heard that human saliva was deadly to centipedes. But this was no ordinary centipede. This was so monstrous that even to think of such a creature made one creep with horror. Hidesato determined to try his last chance. So taking his last arrow and first putting the end of it in his mouth, he fitted the notch to his bow, took careful aim once more and let fly.

This time the arrow again hit the centipede right in the middle of its head, but instead of glancing off harmlessly as before, it struck home to the creature's brain. Then with a convulsive shudder the serpentine body stopped moving, and the fiery light of its great eyes and hundred feet darkened to a dull glare like the sunset of a stormy day, and then went out in blackness. A great darkness now overspread the heavens, the thunder rolled and the lightning flashed, and the wind roared in fury, and it seemed as if the world were coming to an end. The Dragon King and his children and retainers all crouched in different parts of the palace, frightened to death, for the building was shaken to its foundations. At last the dreadful night was over. Day dawned beautiful and clear. The centipede was gone from the mountain.

Then Hidesato called to the Dragon King to come out with him on the balcony, for the centipede was dead and he had nothing more to fear.

Then all the inhabitants of the palace came out with joy, and Hidesato pointed to the lake. There lay the body of the dead centipede floating on the water, which was dyed red with its blood.

The gratitude of the Dragon King knew no bounds. The whole family came and bowed down before the warrior, calling him their preserver and the bravest warrior in all Japan.

Another feast was prepared, more sumptuous than the first. All kinds of fish, prepared in every imaginable way, raw, stewed, boiled and roasted, served on coral trays and crystal dishes, were put before him, and the wine was the best that Hidesato had ever tasted in his life. To add to the beauty of everything the sun shone brightly, the lake glittered like a liquid diamond, and the palace was a thousand times more beautiful by day than by night.

His host tried to persuade the warrior to stay a few days, but Hidesato insisted on going home, saying that he had now finished what he had come to do, and must return. The Dragon King and his family were all very sorry to have him leave so soon, but since he would go they begged him to accept a few small presents (so they said) in token of their gratitude to him for delivering them for ever from their horrible enemy the centipede.

As the warrior stood in the porch taking leave, a train of fish was suddenly transformed into a retinue of men, all wearing ceremonial robes and dragon's crowns on their heads to show that they were servants of the great Dragon King. The presents that they carried were as follows:

First, a large bronze bell.

Second, a bag of rice.

Third, a roll of silk.

Fourth, a cooking pot.

Fifth, a bell.

Hidesato did not want to accept all these presents, but as the Dragon King insisted, he could not well refuse.

The Dragon King himself accompanied the warrior as far as the bridge, and then took leave of him with many bows and good wishes, leaving the procession of servants to accompany Hidesato to his house with the presents.

The warrior's household and servants had been very much concerned when they found that he did not return the night before, but they finally concluded that he had been kept by the violent storm and had taken shelter somewhere. When the

The Procession.

servants on the watch for his return caught sight of him they called to everyone that he was approaching, and the whole household turned out to meet him, wondering much what the retinue of men, bearing presents and banners, that followed him, could mean.

As soon as the Dragon King's retainers had put down the presents they vanished, and Hidesato told all that had happened to him.

The presents which he had received from the grateful Dragon King were found to be of magic power. The bell only was ordinary, and as Hidesato had no use for it he presented it to the temple near by, where it was hung up, to boom out the hour of day over the surrounding neighbourhood.

The single bag of rice, however much was taken from it day after day for the meals of the knight and his whole family, never grew less—the supply in the bag was inexhaustible.

The roll of silk, too, never grew shorter, though time after time long pieces were cut off to make the warrior a new suit of clothes to go to Court in at the New Year.

The cooking pot was wonderful, too. No matter what was put into it, it cooked deliciously whatever was wanted without any firing—truly a very economical saucepan.

The fame of Hidesato's fortune spread far and wide, and as there was no need for him to spend money on rice or silk or firing, he became very rich and prosperous, and was henceforth known as *My Lord Bag of Rice*.

THE TONGUE-CUT SPARROW.

Long, long ago in Japan there lived an old man and his wife. The old man was a good, kind-hearted, hard-working old fellow, but his wife was a regular cross-patch, who spoilt the happiness of her home by her scolding tongue. She was always grumbling about something from morning to night. The old man had for a long time ceased to take any notice of her crossness. He was out most of the day at work in the fields, and as he had no child, for his amusement when he came home, he kept a tame sparrow. He loved the little bird just as much as if she had been his child.

When he came back at night after his hard day's work in the open air it was his only pleasure to pet the sparrow, to talk to her and to teach her little tricks, which she learned very quickly. The old man would open her cage and let her fly about the room, and they would play together. Then when supper-time came, he always saved some tit-bits from his meal with which to feed his little bird.

Now one day the old man went out to chop wood in the forest, and the old woman stopped at home to wash clothes. The day before, she had made some starch, and now when she came to look for it, it was all gone; the bowl which she had filled full yesterday was quite empty.

While she was wondering who could have used or stolen

the starch, down flew the pet sparrow, and bowing her little feathered head—a trick which she had been taught by her master—the pretty bird chirped and said :

"It is I who have taken the starch. I thought it was some food put out for me in that basin, and I ate it all. If I have made a mistake I beg you to forgive me! tweet, tweet, tweet!"

You see from this that the sparrow was a truthful bird, and the old woman ought to have been willing to forgive her at once when she asked her pardon so nicely. But not so.

The old woman had never loved the sparrow, and had often quarrelled with her husband for keeping what she called a dirty bird about the house, saying that it only made extra work for her. Now she was only too delighted to have some cause of complaint against the pet. She scolded and even cursed the poor little bird for her bad behaviour, and not content with using these harsh, unfeeling words, in a fit of rage she seized the sparrow—who all this time had spread out her wings and bowed her head before the old woman, to show how sorry she was—and fetched the scissors and cut off the poor little bird's tongue.

"I suppose you took my starch with that tongue! Now you may see what it is like to go without it!" And with these dreadful words she drove the bird away, not caring in the least what might happen to it and without the smallest pity for its suffering, so unkind was she!

The old woman, after she had driven the sparrow away, made some more rice-paste, grumbling all the time at the

And with these Dreadful Words she drove the Bird away.

trouble, and after starching all her clothes, spread the things on boards to dry in the sun, instead of ironing them as they do in England.

In the evening the old man came home. As usual, on the way back he looked forward to the time when he should reach his gate and see his pet come flying and chirping to meet him, ruffling out her feathers to show her joy, and at last coming to rest on his shoulder. But to-night the old man was very disappointed, for not even the shadow of his dear sparrow was to be seen.

He quickened his steps, hastily drew off his straw sandals, and stepped on to the verandah. Still no sparrow was to be seen. He now felt sure that his wife, in one of her cross tempers, had shut the sparrow up in its cage. So he called her and said anxiously :

" Where is Suzume San (Miss Sparrow) to-day ? "

The old woman pretended not to know at first, and answered :

" Your sparrow ? I am sure I don't know. Now I come to think of it, I haven't seen her all the afternoon. I shouldn't wonder if the ungrateful bird had flown away and left you after all your petting ! "

But at last, when the old man gave her no peace, but asked her again and again, insisting that she must know what had happened to his pet, she confessed all. She told him crossly how the sparrow had eaten the rice-paste she had specially made for starching her clothes, and how when the sparrow had confessed to what she had done, in great anger she had taken her scissors and cut out her tongue, and how finally she had driven the bird away and forbidden her to return to the house again.

Then the old woman showed her husband the sparrow's tongue, saying:

"Here is the tongue I cut off! Horrid little bird, why did it eat all my starch?"

"How could you be so cruel? Oh! how could you be so cruel?" was all that the old man could answer. He was too kind-hearted to punish his shrew of a wife, but he was terribly distressed at what had happened to his poor little sparrow.

"What a dreadful misfortune for my poor Suzume San to lose her tongue!" he said to himself. "She won't be able to chirp any more, and surely the pain of the cutting of it out in that rough way must have made her ill! Is there nothing to be done?"

The old man shed many tears after his cross wife had gone to sleep. While he wiped away the tears with the sleeve of his cotton robe, a bright thought comforted him: he would go and look for the sparrow on the morrow. Having decided this he was able to go to sleep at last.

The next morning he rose early, as soon as ever the day broke, and snatching a hasty breakfast, started out over the hills and through the woods, stopping at every clump of bamboos to cry:

"Where, oh where does my tongue-cut sparrow stay? Where, oh where, does my tongue-cut sparrow stay?"

He never stopped to rest for his noonday meal, and it was far on in the afternoon when he found himself near a large bamboo wood. Bamboo groves are the favourite haunts of sparrows, and there sure enough at the edge of the wood he saw his own dear sparrow waiting to welcome him. He could hardly believe his eyes for joy, and ran forward quickly to greet her. She bowed her little head and went through a number of the tricks her master had taught her, to show her pleasure at seeing her old friend again, and, wonderful to relate, she could talk as of old. The old man told her how sorry he was for all that had happened, and inquired after her tongue, wondering how she could speak so well without it. Then the sparrow opened her beak and showed him that a new tongue had grown in place of the old one, and begged him not to think any more about the past, for she was quite well now. Then the old man knew that his sparrow was a fairy, and no common bird. It would be difficult to exaggerate the old man's rejoicing now. He forgot all his troubles, he forgot even how tired he was, for he had found his lost sparrow, and instead of being ill and without a tongue as he had feared and expected to find her, she was well and happy and with a new tongue, and without a sign of the ill-treatment she had received from his wife. And above all she was a fairy.

The sparrow asked him to follow her, and flying before him she led him to a beautiful house in the heart of the bamboo grove. The old man was utterly astonished when he entered the house to find what a beautiful place it was. It was built of the whitest wood, the soft cream-coloured mats which took the place of carpets were the finest he had ever seen, and the cushions that the sparrow brought out for him to sit on were made of the finest silk and

crape.   Beautiful vases and lacquer boxes adorned the
tokonoma[1] of every room.

The sparrow led the old man to the place of honour, and
then, taking her place at a humble distance, she thanked him

The Lady Sparrow introduced all her Family.

with many polite bows for all the kindness he had shown her
for many long years.

Then the Lady Sparrow, as we will now call her, introduced
all her family to the old man. This done, her daughters, robed in
dainty crape gowns, brought in on beautiful old-fashioned trays
a feast of all kinds of delicious foods, till the old man began to

[1] An alcove where precious objects are displayed.

think he must be dreaming. In the middle of the dinner some of the sparrow's daughters performed a wonderful dance, called the " *Suzume-odori* " or the " Sparrow's dance," to amuse the guest.

Never had the old man enjoyed himself so much. The hours flew by too quickly in this lovely spot, with all these fairy sparrows to wait upon him and to feast him and to dance before him.

But the night came on and the darkness reminded him that he had a long way to go and must think about taking his leave and return home. He thanked his kind hostess for her splendid entertainment, and begged her for his sake to forget all she had suffered at the hands of his cross old wife. He told the Lady Sparrow that it was a great comfort and happiness to him to find her in such a beautiful home and to know that she wanted for nothing. It was his anxiety to know how she fared and what had really happened to her that had led him to seek her. Now he knew that all was well he could return home with a light heart. If ever she wanted him for anything she had only to send for him and he would come at once.

The Lady Sparrow begged him to stay and rest several days and enjoy the change, but the old man said that he must return to his old wife—who would probably be cross at his not coming home at the usual time—and to his work, and therefore, much as he wished to do so, he could not accept her kind invitation. But now that he knew where the Lady Sparrow lived he would come to see her whenever he had the time.

When the Lady Sparrow saw that she could not persuade the old man to stay longer, she gave an order to some of her servants, and they at once brought in two boxes, one large and the other small.   These were placed before the old man, and the Lady Sparrow asked him to choose whichever he liked for a present, which she wished to give him.

The old man could not refuse this kind proposal, and he chose the smaller box, saying:

" I am now too old and feeble to carry the big and heavy box. As you are so kind as to say that I may take whichever I like, I will choose the small one, which will be easier for me to carry."

Then the sparrows all helped him put it on his back and went to the gate to see him off, bidding him good-bye with many bows and entreating him to come again whenever he had the time.   Thus the old man and his pet sparrow separated quite happily, the sparrow showing not the least ill-will for all the unkindness she had suffered at the hands of the old wife. Indeed, she only felt sorrow for the old man who had to put up with it all his life.

When the old man reached home he found his wife even crosser than usual, for it was late on in the night and she had been waiting up for him for a long time.

" Where have you been all this time ? " she asked in a big voice.   " Why do you come back so late ? "

The old man tried to pacify her by showing her the box of presents he had brought back with him, and then he told her of all that had happened to him, and how wonderfully he had been entertained at the sparrow's house.

" Now let us see what is in the box," said the old man, not giving her time to grumble again.   " You must help me open it."   And they both sat down before the box and opened it.

To their utter astonishment they found the box filled to the brim with gold and silver coins and many other precious things. The mats of their little cottage fairly glittered as they took out the things one by one and put them down and handled them over and over again. The old man was overjoyed at the sight of the riches that were now his. Beyond his brightest expectations was the sparrow's gift, which would enable him to give up work and live in ease and comfort the rest of his days.

He said : " Thanks to my good little sparrow ! Thanks to my good little sparrow ! " many times.

But the old woman, after the first moments of surprise and satisfaction at the sight of the gold and silver were over, could not suppress the greed of her wicked nature. She now began to reproach the old man for not having brought home the big box of presents, for in the innocence of his heart he had told her how he had refused the large box of presents which the sparrows had offered him, preferring the smaller one because it was light and easy to carry home.

" You silly old man," said she, " why did you not bring the large box ? Just think what we have lost. We might have had twice as much silver and gold as this. You are certainly an old fool ! " she screamed, and then went to bed as angry as she could be.

The old man now wished that he had said nothing about the big box, but it was too late ; the greedy old woman, not contented with the good luck which had so unexpectedly befallen them and which she so little deserved, made up her mind, if possible, to get more.

Early the next morning she got up and made the old man

describe the way to the sparrow's house. When he saw what
was in her mind he tried to keep her from going, but it was
useless. She would not listen to one word he said. It is
strange that the old woman did not feel ashamed of going to
see the sparrow after the cruel way she had treated her in
cutting off her tongue in a fit of rage. But her greed to get the
big box made her forget everything else. It did not even enter
her thoughts that the sparrows might be angry with her—as,
indeed, they were—and might punish her for what she had done.

Ever since the Lady Sparrow had returned home in the sad
plight in which they had first found her, weeping and bleeding
from the mouth, her whole family and relations had done little
else but speak of the cruelty of the old woman. " How could
she," they asked each other, "inflict such a heavy punishment
for such a trifling offence as that of eating some rice-paste by
mistake ? "   They all loved the old man who was so kind and
good and patient under all his troubles, but the old woman they
hated, and they determined, if ever they had the chance, to
punish her as she deserved. They had not long to wait.

After walking for some hours the old woman had at last
found the bamboo grove which she had made her husband
carefully describe, and now she stood before it crying out :

" Where is the tongue-cut sparrow's house ? Where is the
tongue-cut sparrow's house ? "

At last she saw the eaves of the house peeping out from
amongst the bamboo foliage. She hastened to the door and
knocked loudly.

When the servants told the Lady Sparrow that her old
mistress was at the door asking to see her, she was somewhat

surprised at the unexpected visit, after all that had taken place, and she wondered not a little at the boldness of the old woman in venturing to come to the house. The Lady Sparrow, however, was a polite bird, and so she went out to greet the old woman, remembering that she had once been her mistress.

The old woman intended, however, to waste no time in words, she went right to the point, without the least shame, and said:

"You need not trouble to entertain me as you did my old man. I have come myself to get the box which he so stupidly left behind. I shall soon take my leave if you will give me the big box—that is all I want!"

The Lady Sparrow at once consented, and told her servants to bring out the big box. The old woman eagerly seized it and hoisted it on her back, and without even stopping to thank the Lady Sparrow began to hurry homewards.

The box was so heavy that she could not walk fast, much less run, as she would have liked to do, so anxious was she to get home and see what was inside the box, but she had often to sit down and rest herself by the way.

While she was staggering along under the heavy load, her desire to open the box became too great to be resisted. She could wait no longer, for she supposed this big box to be full of gold and silver and precious jewels like the small one her husband had received.

At last this greedy and selfish old woman put down the box by the wayside and opened it carefully, expecting to gloat her eyes on a mine of wealth. What she saw, however, so terrified her that she nearly lost her senses. As soon as she lifted the

The Old Woman had never been so Frightened in her Life.

lid, a number of horrible and frightful looking demons bounced out of the box and surrounded her as if they intended to kill her. Not even in nightmares had she ever seen such horrible creatures as her much-coveted box contained. A demon with one huge eye right in the middle of its forehead came and glared at her, monsters with gaping mouths looked as if they would devour her, a huge snake coiled and hissed about her, and a big frog hopped and croaked towards her.

The old woman had never been so frightened in her life, and ran from the spot as fast as her quaking legs would carry her, glad to escape alive. When she reached home she fell to the floor and told her husband with tears all that had happened to her, and how she had been nearly killed by the demons in the box.

Then she began to blame the sparrow, but the old man stopped her at once, saying:

" Don't blame the sparrow, it is your wickedness which has at last met with its reward. I only hope this may be a lesson to you in the future ! "

The old woman said nothing more, and from that day she repented of her cross, unkind ways, and by degrees became a good old woman, so that her husband hardly knew her to be the same person, and they spent their last days together happily, free from want or care, spending carefully the treasure the old man had received from his pet, the tongue-cut sparrow.

THE STORY OF URASHIMA TARO, THE FISHER LAD.

Long, long ago in the province of Tango there lived on the shore of Japan in the little fishing village of Mizu-no-ye a young fisherman named Urashima Taro. His father had been a fisherman before him, and his skill had more than doubly descended to his son, for Urashima was the most skilful fisher in all that country side, and could catch more *bonito* and *tai* in a day than his comrades could in a week.

But in the little fishing village, more than for being a clever fisher of the sea was he known for his kind heart. In his whole life he had never hurt anything, either great or small, and when a boy, his companions had always laughed at him, for he would never join with them in teasing animals, but always tried to keep them from this cruel sport.

One soft summer twilight he was going home at the end of a day's fishing when he came upon a group of children. They were all screaming and talking at the tops of their voices, and seemed to be in a state of great excitement about something, and on his going up to them to see what was the matter he saw that they were tormenting a tortoise. First one boy pulled it this way, then another boy pulled it that way, while a third child beat it with a stick, and the fourth hammered its shell with a stone.

Now Urashima felt very sorry for the poor tortoise and made up his mind to rescue it.   He spoke to the boys :

" Look here, boys, you are treating that poor tortoise so badly that it will soon die ! "

The boys, who were all of an age when children seem to delight in being cruel to animals, took no notice of Urashima's gentle reproof, but went on teasing it as before.   One of the older boys answered :

" Who cares whether it lives or dies ?   We do not.   Here, boys, go on, go on ! "

And they began to treat the poor tortoise more cruelly than ever.   Urashima waited a moment, turning over in his mind what would be the best way to deal with the boys.   He would try to persuade them to give the tortoise up to him, so he smiled at them and said :

" I am sure you are all good, kind boys !   Now won't you give me the tortoise ?   I should like to have it so much ! "

" No, we won't give you the tortoise," said one of the boys. " Why should we ?   We caught it ourselves."

" What you say is true," said Urashima, " but I do not ask you to give it to me for nothing.   I will give you some money for it—in other words, the Ojisan (Uncle) will buy it of you. Won't that do for you, my boys ? "   He held up the money to them, strung on a piece of string through a hole in the centre of each coin.   " Look, boys, you can buy anything you like with this money.   You can do much more with this money than you can with that poor tortoise.   See what good boys you are to listen to me."

The boys were not bad boys at all, they were only

mischievous, and as Urashima spoke they were won by his kind smile and gentle words and began "to be of his spirit," as they say in Japan. Gradually they all came up to him, the ringleader of the little band holding out the tortoise to him.

" Very well, Ojisan, we will give you the tortoise if you will give us the money ! " And Urashima took the tortoise and gave the money to the boys, who, calling to each other, scampered away and were soon out of sight.

Then Urashima stroked the tortoise's back, saying as he did so :

" Oh, you poor thing ! Poor thing!—there, there! you are safe now ! They say that a stork lives for a thousand years, but the tortoise for ten thousand years. You have the longest life of any creature in this world, and you were in great danger of having that precious life cut short by those cruel boys. Luckily I was passing by and saved you, and so life is still yours. Now I am going to take you back to your home, the sea, at once. Do not let yourself be caught again, for there might be no one to save you next time ! "

All the time that the kind fisherman was speaking he was walking quickly to the shore and out upon the rocks ; then putting the tortoise into the water he watched the animal disappear, and turned homewards himself, for he was tired and the sun had set.

The next morning Urashima went out as usual in his boat. The weather was fine and the sea and sky were both blue and soft in the tender haze of the summer morning. Urashima got into his boat and dreamily pushed out to sea, throwing his line as he did so.   He soon passed the other fishing boats and left them behind him till they were lost to sight in the distance, and his boat drifted further and further out upon the blue waters. Somehow, he knew not why, he felt unusually happy that morning; and he could not help wishing that, like the tortoise he set free the day before, he had thousands of years to live instead of his own short span of human life.

He was suddenly startled from his reverie by hearing his own name called:

" Urashima, Urashima ! "

Clear as a bell and soft as the summer wind the name floated over the sea.

He stood up and looked in every direction, thinking that one of the other boats had overtaken him, but gaze as he might over the wide expanse of water, near or far there was no sign of a boat, so the voice could not have come from any human being.

Startled, and wondering who or what it was that had called him so clearly, he looked in all directions round about him and saw that without his knowing it a tortoise had come to the side of the boat.   Urashima saw with surprise that it was the very tortoise he had rescued the day before.

" Well, Mr. Tortoise," said Urashima, "was it you who called my name just now ? "

The tortoise nodded its head several times, and said :

" Yes, it was I.   Yesterday in your honourable shadow (*o kage sama de*) my life was saved, and I have come to offer you my thanks and to tell you how grateful I am for your kindness to me."

"Indeed," said Urashima, "that is very polite of you. Come up into the boat. I would offer you a smoke, but as you are a tortoise doubtless you do not smoke," and the fisherman laughed at the joke.

"He—he—he—he!" laughed the tortoise; "*sake* (rice wine) is my favourite refreshment, but I do not care for tobacco."

"Indeed," said Urashima, "I regret very much that I have no '*sake*' in my boat to offer you, but come up and dry your back in the sun—tortoises always love to do that."

So the tortoise climbed into the boat, the fisherman helping him, and after an exchange of complimentary speeches the tortoise said :

"Have you ever seen Rin Gin, the Palace of the Dragon King of the Sea, Urashima ?"

The fisherman shook his head and replied : "No ; year after year the sea has been my home, but though I have often heard of the Dragon King's realm under the sea I have never yet set eyes on that wonderful place. It must be very far away, if it exists at all ! "

"Is that really so ? You have never seen the Sea King's Palace ? Then you have missed seeing one of the most wonderful sights in the whole universe. It is far away at the bottom of the sea, but if I take you there we shall soon reach the place. If you would like to see the Sea King's land I will be your guide."

"I should like to go there, certainly, and you are very kind to think of taking me, but you must remember that I am only a poor mortal and have not the power of swimming like a sea creature such as you are——"

Before the fisherman could say more the tortoise stopped him, saying :

" What ? You need not swim yourself.   If you will ride on my back I will take you without any trouble on your part."

" But," said Urashima, " how is it possible for me to ride on your small back ? "

" It may seem absurd to you, but I assure you that you can do so.   Try at once !   Just come and get on my back, and see if it is as impossible as you think ! "

As the tortoise finished speaking, Urashima looked at its shell, and strange to say he saw that the creature had suddenly grown so big that a man could easily sit on its back.

" This is strange indeed ! " said Urashima ; " then, Mr. Tortoise, with your kind permission I will get on your back. *Dokoisho !* " [1] he exclaimed as he jumped on.

The tortoise, with an unmoved face, as if this strange proceeding were quite an ordinary event, said :

" Now we will set out at our leisure," and with these words he leapt into the sea with Urashima on his back.   Down through the water the tortoise dived.   For a long time these two strange companions rode through the sea.   Urashima never grew tired, nor his clothes moist with the water.   At last, far away in the distance a magnificent gate appeared, and behind the gate, the long, sloping roofs of a palace on the horizon.

" Ya," exclaimed Urashima, " that looks like the gate of some large palace just appearing !   Mr. Tortoise, can you tell what that place is we can now see ? "

" That is the great gate of the Rin Gin Palace.   The large

[1] " All right " (only used by lower classes).

roof that you see behind the gate is the Sea King's Palace itself."

"Then we have at last come to the realm of the Sea King and to his Palace," said Urashima.

"Yes, indeed," answered the tortoise, "and don't you think

The Gate of some large Palace.

we have come very quickly?" And while he was speaking the tortoise reached the side of the gate. "And here we are, and you must please walk from here."

The tortoise now went in front, and speaking to the gate-keeper said:

"This is Urashima Taro, from the country of Japan. I

have had the honour of bringing him as a visitor to this kingdom. Please show him the way."

Then the gatekeeper, who was a fish, at once led the way through the gate before them.

The red bream, the flounder, the sole, the cuttlefish, and all the chief vassals of the Dragon King of the Sea now came out with courtly bows to welcome the stranger.

"Urashima Sama, Urashima Sama! welcome to the Sea Palace, the home of the Dragon King of the Sea. Thrice welcome are you, having come from such a distant country. And you, Mr. Tortoise, we are greatly indebted to you for all your trouble in bringing Urashima here." Then, turning again to Urashima, they said, " Please follow us this way," and from here the whole band of fishes became his guides.

Urashima, being only a poor fisher lad, did not know how to behave in a palace ; but, strange though it all was to him, he did not feel ashamed or embarrassed, but followed his kind guides quite calmly where they led to the inner palace. When he reached the portals a beautiful Princess with her attendant maidens came out to welcome him. She was more beautiful than any human being, and was robed in flowing garments of red and soft green like the under side of a wave, and golden threads glimmered through the folds of her gown. Her lovely black hair streamed over her shoulders in the fashion of a king's daughter many hundreds of years ago, and when she spoke her voice sounded like music over the water. Urashima was lost in wonder while he looked upon her, and he could not speak. Then he remembered that he ought to bow, but before he could make a low obeisance the Princess took him by the hand and led him to a beautiful hall, and to the seat of honour at the upper end, and bade him be seated.

"Urashima Taro, it gives me the highest pleasure to welcome you to my father's kingdom," said the Princess. "Yesterday you set free a tortoise, and I have sent for you to thank you for saving my life, for I was that tortoise. Now if you like you shall live here for ever in the land of eternal youth, where summer never dies and where sorrow never comes, and I will be your bride if you will, and we will live together happily for ever afterwards!"

And as Urashima listened to her sweet words and gazed upon her lovely face his heart was filled with a great wonder and joy, and he answered her, wondering if it was not all a dream:

"Thank you a thousand times for your kind speech. There is nothing I could wish for more than to be permitted to stay here with you in this beautiful land, of which I have often heard, but have never seen to this day. Beyond all words, this is the most wonderful place I have ever seen."

While he was speaking a train of fishes appeared, all dressed in ceremonial, trailing garments. One by one, silently and with stately steps, they entered the hall, bearing on coral trays delicacies of fish and seaweed, such as no one can dream of, and this wondrous feast was set before the bride and bridegroom. The bridal was celebrated with dazzling splendour, and in the Sea King's realm there was great rejoicing. As soon as the young pair had pledged themselves in the wedding cup of wine, three times three, music was played, and songs were sung, and fishes with silver scales and golden tails stepped in from the waves and danced. Urashima enjoyed

Urashima Taro and the Sea King's Daughter.

himself with all his heart.   Never in his whole life had he sat down to such a marvellous feast.

When the feast was over the Princess asked the bridegroom if he would like to walk through the palace and see all there was to be seen.   Then the happy fisherman, following his bride, the Sea King's daughter, was shown all the wonders of that enchanted land where youth and joy go hand in hand and neither time nor age can touch them.   The palace was built of coral and adorned with pearls, and the beauties and wonders of the place were so great that the tongue fails to describe them.

But, to Urashima, more wonderful than the palace was the garden that surrounded it.   Here was to be seen at one time the scenery of the four different seasons ; the beauties of summer and winter, spring and autumn, were displayed to the wondering visitor at once.

First, when he looked to the east, the plum and cherry trees were seen in full bloom, the nightingales sang in the pink avenues, and butterflies flitted from flower to flower.

Looking to the south all the trees were green in the fulness of summer, and the day cicala and the night cricket chirruped loudly.

Looking to the west the autumn maples were ablaze like a sunset sky, and the chrysanthemums were in perfection.

Looking to the north the change made Urashima start, for the ground was silver white with snow, and trees and bamboos were also covered with snow and the pond was thick with ice.

And each day there were new joys and new wonders for

Urashima, and so great was his happiness that he forgot everything, even the home he had left behind and his parents and his own country, and three days passed without his even thinking of all he had left behind. Then his mind came back to him and he remembered who he was, and that he did not belong to this wonderful land or the Sea King's palace, and he said to himself:

"O dear! I must not stay on here, for I have an old father and mother at home. What can have happened to them all this time? How anxious they must have been these days when I did not return as usual. I must go back at once without letting one more day pass." And he began to prepare for the journey in great haste.

Then he went to his beautiful wife, the Princess, and bowing low before her he said:

"Indeed, I have been very happy with you for a long time, Otohime Sama" (for that was her name), "and you have been kinder to me than any words can tell. But now I must say good-bye. I must go back to my old parents."

Then Otohime Sama began to weep, and said softly and sadly:

"Is it not well with you here, Urashima, that you wish to leave me so soon? Where is the haste? Stay with me yet another day only!"

But Urashima had remembered his old parents, and in Japan the duty to parents is stronger than everything else, stronger even than pleasure or love, and he would not be persuaded, but answered:

"Indeed, I must go. Do not think that I wish to leave

you.   It is not that.   I must go and see my old parents.   Let
me go for one day and I will come back to you."

"Then," said the Princess sorrowfully, "there is nothing
to be done.   I will send you back to-day to your father and
mother, and instead of trying to keep you with me one more
day, I shall give you this as a token of our love—please take
it back with you"; and she brought him a beautiful lacquer box
tied about with a silken cord and tassels of red silk.

Urashima had received so much from the Princess already
that he felt some compunction in taking the gift, and said:

"It does not seem right for me to take yet another gift
from you after all the many favours I have received at your
hands, but because it is your wish I will do so," and then
he added:

"Tell me what is this box?"

"That," answered the Princess "is the *Tamate-Bako* (Box
of the Jewel Hand), and it contains something very precious.
You must not open this box, whatever happens!   If you open
it something dreadful will happen to you!   Now promise me
that you will never open this box!"

And Urashima promised that he would never, *never* open
the box whatever happened.

Then bidding good-bye to Otohime Sama he went down to
the seashore, the Princess and her attendants following him,
and there he found a large tortoise waiting for him.

He quickly mounted the creature's back and was carried
away over the shining sea into the East.   He looked back to
wave his hand to Otohime Sama till at last he could see her
no more, and the land of the Sea King and the roofs of the

wonderful palace were lost in the far, far distance. Then, with his face turned eagerly towards his own land, he looked for the rising of the blue hills on the horizon before him.

At last the tortoise carried him into the bay he knew so well, and to the shore from whence he had set out. He stepped on to the shore and looked about him while the tortoise rode away back to the Sea King's realm.

But what is the strange fear that seizes Urashima as he stands and looks about him ? Why does he gaze so fixedly at the people that pass him by, and why do they in turn stand and look at him ? The shore is the same and the hills are the same, but the people that he sees walking past him have very different faces to those he had known so well before.

Wondering what it can mean he walks quickly towards his old home. Even that looks different, but a house stands on the spot, and he calls out:

" Father, I have just returned !" and he was about to enter, when he saw a strange man coming out.

" Perhaps my parents have moved while I have been away, and have gone somewhere else," was the fisherman's thought. Somehow he began to feel strangely anxious, he could not tell why.

" Excuse me," said he to the man who was staring at him, " but till within the last few days I have lived in this house. My name is Urashima Taro. Where have my parents gone whom I left here ?"

A very bewildered expression came over the face of the man, and, still gazing intently on Urashima's face, he said:

" What ? Are you Urashima Taro ?"

" Yes," said the fisherman, " I am Urashima Taro ! "

" Ha, ha ! " laughed the man, " you must not make such jokes.   It is true that once upon a time a man called Urashima Taro did live in this village, but that is a story three hundred years old.   He could not possibly be alive now ! "

When Urashima heard these strange words he was frightened, and said :

" Please, please, you must not joke with me, for I am greatly perplexed.   I am really Urashima Taro, and I certainly have not lived three hundred years.   Till four or five days ago I lived on this spot.   Tell me what I want to know without more joking, please."

But the man's face grew more and more grave, and he answered :

" You may or may not be Urashima Taro, I don't know. But the Urashima Taro of whom I have heard is a man who lived three hundred years ago.   Perhaps you are his spirit come to re-visit your old home ? "

" Why do you mock me ? " said Urashima.   " I am no spirit !   I am a living man—do you not see my feet " ; and " don-don," he stamped on the ground, first with one foot and then with the other to show the man.   (Japanese ghosts have no feet.)

" But Urashima Taro lived three hundred years ago, that is all I know ; it is written in the village chronicles," persisted the man, who could not believe what the fisherman said.

Urashima was lost in bewilderment and trouble.   He stood looking all around him, terribly puzzled, and, indeed, something in the appearance of everything was different to what he remembered before he went away, and the awful feeling came over him that what the man said was perhaps true. He seemed to be in a strange dream. The few days he

A beautiful little Purple Cloud rose out of the Box.

had spent in the Sea King's palace beyond the sea had not been days at all; they had been hundreds of years, and in that time his parents had died and all the people he had ever known, and the village had written down his story. There was no use in staying here any longer. He must get back to his beautiful wife beyond the sea.

He made his way back to the beach, carrying in his hand the box which the Princess had given him. But which was the way ? He could not find it alone ! Suddenly he remembered the box, the *Tamate-Bako.*

" The Princess told me when she gave me the box never to open it—that it contained a very precious thing. But now that I have no home, now that I have lost everything that was dear to me here, and my heart grows thin with sadness, at such a time, if I open the box, surely I shall find something that will help me, something that will show me the way back to my beautiful Princess over the sea. There is nothing else for me to do now. Yes, yes, I will open the box and look in ! "

And so his heart consented to this act of disobedience, and he tried to persuade himself that he was doing the right thing in breaking his promise.

Slowly, very slowly, he untied the red silk cord, slowly and wonderingly he lifted the lid of the precious box. And what did he find ? Strange to say only a beautiful little purple cloud rose out of the box in three soft wisps. For an instant it covered his face and wavered over him as if loth to go, and then it floated away like vapour over the sea.

Urashima, who had been till that moment like a strong and handsome youth of twenty-four, suddenly became very, very old. His back doubled up with age, his hair turned snowy white, his face wrinkled and he fell down dead on the beach.

Poor Urashima ! because of his disobedience he could never return to the Sea King's realm or the lovely Princess beyond the sea.

Little children, never be disobedient to those who are wiser than you, for disobedience was the beginning of all the miseries and sorrows of life.

THE FARMER AND THE BADGER.

LONG, long ago, there lived an old farmer and his wife who had made their home in the mountains, far from any town. Their only neighbour was a bad and malicious badger. This badger used to come out every night and run across to the farmer's field and spoil the vegetables and the rice which the farmer spent his time in carefully cultivating. The badger at last grew so ruthless in his mischievous work, and did so much harm everywhere on the farm, that the good-natured farmer could not stand it any longer, and determined to put a stop to it. So he lay in wait day after day and night after night, with a big club, hoping to catch the badger, but all in vain. Then he laid traps for the wicked animal.

The farmer's trouble and patience was rewarded, for one fine day on going his rounds he found the badger caught in a hole he had dug for that purpose. The farmer was delighted at having caught his enemy, and carried him home securely bound with rope. When he reached the house the farmer said to his wife :

" I have at last caught the bad badger. You must keep an eye on him while I am out at work and not let him escape, because I want to make him into soup to-night."

Saying this, he hung the badger up to the rafters of his storehouse and went out to his work in the fields. The badger

The Farmer's Wife pounding Barley.

was in great distress, for he did not at all like the idea of being made into soup that night, and he thought and thought for a long time, trying to hit upon some plan by which he might escape. It was hard to think clearly in his uncomfortable position, for he had been hung upside down. Very near him, at the entrance to the storehouse, looking out towards the green fields and the trees and the pleasant sunshine, stood the farmer's old wife pounding barley. She looked tired and old. Her face was seamed with many wrinkles, and was as brown as leather, and every now and then she stopped to wipe the perspiration which rolled down her face.

"Dear lady," said the wily badger, "you must be very weary doing such heavy work in your old age. Won't you let me do that for you? My arms are very strong, and I could relieve you for a little while!"

"Thank you for your kindness," said the old woman, "but I cannot let you do this work for me because I must not untie you, for you might escape if I did, and my husband would be very angry if he came home and found you gone."

Now, the badger is one of the most cunning of animals, and he said again in a very sad, gentle, voice:

"You are very unkind. You might untie me, for I promise not to try to escape. If you are afraid of your husband, I will let you bind me again before his return when I have finished pounding the barley. I am so tired and sore tied up like this. If you would only let me down for a few minutes I would indeed be thankful!"

The old woman had a good and simple nature, and could not think badly of anyone. Much less did she think that the

badger was only deceiving her in order to get away. She felt
sorry, too, for the animal as she turned to look at him. He
looked in such a sad plight hanging downwards from the ceiling
by his legs, which were all tied together so tightly that the rope
and the knots were cutting into the skin. So in the kindness
of her heart, and believing the creature's promise that he would
not run away, she untied the cord and let him down.

The old woman then gave him the wooden pestle and told
him to do the work for a short time while she rested. He took
the pestle, but instead of doing the work as he was told, the
badger at once sprang upon the old woman and knocked her
down with the heavy piece of wood. He then killed her and
cut her up and made soup of her, and waited for the return of the
old farmer. The old man worked hard in his fields all day,
and as he worked he thought with pleasure that no more now
would his labour be spoiled by the destructive badger.

Towards sunset he left his work and turned to go home.
He was very tired, but the thought of the nice supper of
hot badger soup awaiting his return cheered him. The
thought that the badger might get free and take revenge on
the poor old woman never once came into his mind.

The badger meanwhile assumed the old woman's form, and
as soon as he saw the old farmer approaching came out to greet
him on the verandah of the little house, saying :

" So you have come back at last. I have made the badger
soup and have been waiting for you for a long time."

The old farmer quickly took off his straw sandals and sat
down before his tiny dinner-tray. The innocent man never
even dreamt that it was not his wife but the badger who was

waiting upon him, and asked at once for the soup. Then the badger suddenly transformed himself back to his natural form and cried out :

" You wife-eating old man ! Look out for the bones in the kitchen ! "

Laughing loudly and derisively he escaped out of the house and ran away to his den in the hills. The old man was left behind alone. He could hardly believe what he had seen and heard. Then when he understood the whole truth he was so scared and horrified that he fainted right away. After a while he came round and burst into tears. He cried loudly and bitterly. He rocked himself to and fro in his hopeless grief. It seemed too terrible to be real that his faithful old wife had been killed and cooked by the badger while he was working quietly in the fields, knowing nothing of what was going on at home, and congratulating himself on having once for all got rid of the wicked animal who had so often spoiled his fields. And oh ! the horrible thought; he had very nearly drunk the soup which the creature had made of his poor old woman. "Oh dear, oh dear, oh dear ! " he wailed aloud. Now, not far away there lived in the same mountain a kind, good-natured old rabbit. He heard the old man crying and sobbing and at once set out to see what was the matter, and if there was anything he could do to help his neighbour. The old man told him all that had happened. When the rabbit heard the story he was very angry at the wicked and deceitful badger, and told the old man to leave everything to him and he would avenge his wife's death. The farmer was at last comforted, and, wiping away his tears, thanked the rabbit for his goodness in coming to him in his distress.

The rabbit, seeing that the farmer was growing calmer, went back to his home to lay his plans for the punishment of the badger.

The next day the weather was fine, and the rabbit went out to find the badger. He was not to be seen in the woods or on the hillside or in the fields anywhere, so the rabbit went to his den and found the badger hiding there, for the animal had been afraid to show himself ever since he had escaped from the farmer's house, for fear of the old man's wrath.

The rabbit called out:

"Why are you not out on such a beautiful day? Come out with me, and we will go and cut grass on the hills together."

The badger, never doubting but that the rabbit was his friend, willingly consented to go out with him, only too glad to get away from the neighbourhood of the farmer and the fear of meeting him. The rabbit led the way miles away from their homes, out on the hills where the grass grew tall and thick and sweet. They both set to work to cut down as much as they could carry home, to store it up for their winter's food. When they had each cut down all they wanted they tied it in bundles and then started homewards, each carrying his bundle of grass on his back. This time the rabbit made the badger go first.

When they had gone a little way the rabbit took out a flint and steel, and, striking it over the badger's back as he stepped along in front, set his bundle of grass on fire. The badger heard the flint striking, and asked:

"What is that noise, 'Crack, crack'?"

"Oh, that is nothing," replied the rabbit; "I only said

Set the Bundle of Grass on Fire.

'Crack, crack' because this mountain is called Crackling Mountain.

The fire soon spread in the bundle of dry grass on the badger's back. The badger, hearing the crackle of the burning grass, asked "What is that?"

"Now we have come to the 'Burning Mountain,'" answered the rabbit.

By this time the bundle was nearly burnt out and all the hair had been burnt off the badger's back. He now knew what had happened by the smell of the smoke of the burning grass. Screaming with pain the badger ran as fast as he could to his hole. The rabbit followed and found him lying on his bed groaning with pain.

"What an unlucky fellow you are!" said the rabbit. "I can't imagine how this happened! I will bring you some medicine which will heal your back quickly!"

The rabbit went away glad and smiling to think that the punishment upon the badger had already begun. He hoped that the badger would die of his burns, for he felt that nothing could be too bad for the animal, who was guilty of murdering a poor helpless old woman who had trusted him. He went home and made an ointment by mixing some sauce and red pepper together.

He carried this to the badger, but before putting it on he told him that it would cause him great pain, but that he must bear it patiently, because it was a very wonderful medicine for burns and scalds and such wounds. The badger thanked him and begged him to apply it at once. But no language can describe the agony of the badger as soon as the red pepper had been pasted all over his sore back. He rolled over and over and howled loudly. The rabbit, looking on, felt that the farmer's wife was beginning to be avenged.

The badger was in bed for about a month; but at last, in spite of the red pepper application, his burns healed and he got well. When the rabbit saw that the badger was getting well, he thought of another plan by which he could compass the creature's death. So he went one day to pay the badger a visit and to congratulate him on his recovery.

During the conversation the rabbit mentioned that he was going fishing, and described how pleasant fishing was when the weather was fine and the sea smooth.

The badger listened with pleasure to the rabbit's account of the way he passed his time now, and forgot all his pains and his month's illness, and thought what fun it would be if he could go fishing too; so he asked the rabbit if he would take him the next time he went out to fish. This was just what the rabbit wanted, so he agreed.

Then he went home and built two boats, one of wood and the other of clay. At last they were both finished, and as the rabbit stood and looked at his work he felt that all his trouble would be well rewarded if his plan succeeded, and he could manage to kill the wicked badger now.

The day came when the rabbit had arranged to take the badger fishing. He kept the wooden boat himself and gave the badger the clay boat. The badger, who knew nothing about boats, was delighted with his new boat and thought how kind it was of the rabbit to give it to him. They both got into their boats and set out. After going some distance from the

shore the rabbit proposed that they should try their boats and
see which one could go the quickest. The badger fell in with
the proposal, and they both set to work to row as fast as they

He raised his Oar and Struck at the Badger with all his Strength.

could for some time. In the middle of the race the badger
found his boat going to pieces, for the water now began to
soften the clay. He cried out in great fear to the rabbit to

help him.   But the rabbit answered that he was avenging the old woman's murder, and that this had been his intention all along, and that he was happy to think that the badger had at last met his deserts for all his evil crimes, and was to drown with no one to help him.   Then he raised his oar and struck at the badger with all his strength till he fell with the sinking clay boat and was seen no more.

Thus at last he kept his promise to the old farmer.   The rabbit now turned and rowed shorewards, and having landed and pulled his boat upon the beach, hurried back to tell the old farmer everything, and how the badger, his enemy, had been killed.

The old farmer thanked him with tears in his eyes.   He said that till now he could never sleep at night or be at peace in the daytime, thinking of how his wife's death was unavenged, but from this time he would be able to sleep and eat as of old.   He begged the rabbit to stay with him and share his home, so from this day the rabbit went to stay with the old farmer and they both lived together as good friends to the end of their days.

THE *SHINANSHA*, OR THE SOUTH POINTING CARRIAGE.

THE compass, with its needle always pointing to the North, is quite a common thing, and no one thinks that it is remarkable now, though when it was first invented it must have been a wonder.

Now long ago in China, there was a still more wonderful invention called the *Shinansha*. This was a kind of chariot with the figure of a man on it always pointing to the South. No matter how the chariot was placed the figure always wheeled about and pointed to the South.

This curious instrument was invented by Kotei, one of the three Chinese Emperors of the mythological age. Kotei was the son of the Emperor Yuhi. Before he was born his mother had a vision which foretold that her son would be a great man.

One summer evening she went out to walk in the meadows to seek the cool breezes which blow at the end of the day and to gaze with pleasure at the star-lit heavens above her. As she looked at the North Star, strange to relate, it shot forth vivid flashes of lightning in every direction. Soon after this her son Kotei came into the world.

Kotei in time grew to manhood and succeeded his father the Emperor Yuhi. His early reign was greatly troubled by the rebel Shiyu. This rebel wanted to make himself King, and many were the battles which he fought to this end.   Shiyu was a wicked magician, his head was made of iron, and there was no man that could conquer him.

At last Kotei declared war against the rebel and led his army to battle, and the two armies met on a plain called

He Thought and Pondered Deeply.

Takuroku.   The Emperor boldly attacked the enemy, but the magician brought down a dense fog upon the battlefield, and while the royal army were wandering about in confusion, trying to find their way, Shiyu retreated with his troops, laughing at having fooled the royal army.

No matter however strong and brave the Emperor's

soldiers were, the rebel with his magic could always escape in the end.

Kotei returned to his Palace, and thought and pondered deeply as to how he should conquer the magician, for he was determined not to give up yet. After a long time he invented the *Shinansha* with the figure of a man always pointing South, for there were no compasses in those days. With this instrument to show him the way he need not fear the dense fogs raised up by the magician to confound his men.

Kotei again declared war against Shiyu. He placed the *Shinansha* in front of his army and led the way to the battlefield.

The battle began in earnest. The rebel was being driven backward by the royal troops when he again resorted to magic, and upon his saying some strange words in a loud voice, immediately a dense fog came down upon the battlefield.

But this time no soldier minded the fog, not one was confused. Kotei by pointing to the *Shinansha* could find his way and directed the army without a single mistake. He closely pursued the rebel army and drove them backward till they came to a big river. This river Kotei and his men found was swollen by the floods and impossible to cross.

Shiyu by using his magic art quickly passed over with his army and shut himself up in a fortress on the opposite bank.

When Kotei found his march checked he was wild with disappointment, for he had very nearly overtaken the rebel when the river stopped him.

He could do nothing, for there were no boats in those days, so the Emperor ordered his tent to be pitched in the pleasantest spot that the place afforded.

One day he stepped forth from his tent and after walking about for a short time he came to a pond. Here he sat down on the bank and was lost in thought.

It was autumn. The trees growing along the edge of the water were shedding their leaves, which floated hither and thither on the surface of the pond. By-and-bye, Kotei's attention was attracted to a spider on the brink of the water. The little insect was trying to get on to one of the floating leaves near by. It did so at last, and was soon floating over the water to the other side of the pond.

This little incident made the clever Emperor think that he might try to make something that could carry himself and his men over the river in the same way that the leaf had carried over the spider. He set to work and persevered till he invented the first boat. When he found that it was a success he set all his men to make more, and in time there were enough boats for the whole army.

Kotei now took his army across the river, and attacked Shiyu's headquarters. He gained a complete victory, and so put an end to the war which had troubled his country for so long.

This wise and good Emperor did not rest till he had secured peace and prosperity throughout his whole land. He was beloved by his subjects, who now enjoyed their happiness of peace for many long years under him. He spent a great deal of time in making inventions which would benefit his people, and he succeeded in many besides the boat and the South Pointing *Shinansha*.

He had reigned about a hundred years when one day, as

Kotei was looking upwards, the sky became suddenly red, and
something came glittering like gold towards the earth. As it
came nearer Kotei saw that it was a great Dragon. The Dragon
approached and bowed down its head before the Emperor.

He Mounted the Dragon.

The Empress and the courtiers were so frightened that they
ran away screaming.

But the Emperor only smiled and called to them to stop,
and said:

"Do not be afraid. This is a messenger from Heaven.
My time here is finished!" He then mounted the Dragon,
which began to ascend towards the sky.

When the Empress and the courtiers saw this they all cried out together :

"Wait a moment ! We wish to come too."   And they all ran and caught hold of the Dragon's beard and tried to mount him.

But it was impossible for so many people to ride on the Dragon. Several of them hung on to the creature's beard so that when it tried to mount the hair was pulled out and they fell to the ground.

Meanwhile the Empress and a few of the courtiers were safely seated on the Dragon's back. The Dragon flew up so high in the heavens that in a short time the inmates of the Palace, who had been left behind disappointed, could see them no more.

After some time a bow and an arrow dropped to the earth in the courtyard of the Palace. They were recognised as having belonged to the Emperor Kotei. The courtiers took them up carefully and preserved them as sacred relics in the Palace.

THE ADVENTURES OF KINTARO, THE GOLDEN BOY.

Long, long ago there lived in Kyoto a brave soldier named Kintoki. Now he fell in love with a beautiful lady and married her. Not long after this, through the malice of some of his friends, he fell into disgrace at Court and was dismissed. This misfortune so preyed upon his mind that he did not long survive his dismissal—he died, leaving behind him his beautiful young wife to face the world alone. Fearing her husband's enemies, she fled to the Ashigara Mountains as soon as her husband was dead, and there in the lonely forests where no one ever came except woodcutters, a little boy was born to her. She called him Kintaro or the Golden Boy. Now the remarkable thing about this child was his great strength, and as he grew older he grew stronger and stronger, so that by the time he was eight years of age he was able to cut down trees as quickly as the woodcutters. Then his mother gave him a large axe, and he used to go out in the forest and help the woodcutters, who called him " Wonder-child," and his mother the " Old Nurse of the Mountains," for they did not know her high rank. Another favourite pastime of Kintaro's was to smash up rocks and stones. You can imagine how strong he was !

Quite unlike other boys, Kintaro grew up all alone in the mountain wilds, and as he had no companions he made friends with all the animals and learned to understand them and to speak their strange talk.   By degrees they all grew quite tame and looked upon Kintaro as their master, and he used them as his servants and messengers.   But his special retainers were the bear, the deer, the monkey and the hare.

The bear often brought her cubs for Kintaro to romp with, and when she came to take them home Kintaro would get on her back and have a ride to her cave.   He was very fond of the deer too, and would often put his arms round the creature's neck to show that its long horns did not frighten him.   Great was the fun they all had together.

One day, as usual, Kintaro went up into the mountains, followed by the bear, the deer, the monkey, and the hare. After walking for some time up hill and down dale and over rough roads, they suddenly came out upon a wide and grassy plain covered with pretty wild flowers.

Here, indeed, was a nice place where they could all have a good romp together.   The deer rubbed his horns against a tree for pleasure, the monkey scratched his back, the hare smoothed his long ears, and the bear gave a grunt of satisfaction.

Kintaro said, " Here is a place for a good game.   What do you all say to a wrestling match ? "

The bear being the biggest and the oldest, answered for the others :

" That will be great fun," said she.   " I am the strongest animal, so I will make the platform for the wrestlers "; and she set to work with a will to dig up the earth and to pat it into shape.

" All right," said Kintaro, " I will look on while you all wrestle with each other.   I shall give a prize to the one who wins in each round."

Then the Monkey and the Hare hopped out.

" What fun ! we shall all try to get the prize," said the bear.

The deer, the monkey and the hare set to work to help the bear raise the platform on which they were all to wrestle. When this was finished, Kintaro cried out :

" Now begin ! the monkey and the hare shall open the sports and the deer shall be umpire.   Now, Mr. Deer, you are to be umpire ! "

" He, he ! " answered the deer.   " I will be umpire.   Now, Mr. Monkey and Mr. Hare, if you are both ready, please walk out and take your places on the platform."

Then the monkey and the hare both hopped out, quickly and nimbly, to the wrestling platform.   The deer, as umpire, stood between the two and called out :

" Red-back ! Red-back ! " (this to the monkey, who has a red back in Japan).   " Are you ready ? "

Then he turned to the hare :

" Long-ears ! Long-ears ! are you ready ? "

Both the little wrestlers faced each other while the deer raised a leaf on high as signal.   When he dropped the leaf the monkey and the hare rushed upon each other, crying "Yoisho, yoisho ! "

While the monkey and the hare wrestled, the deer called out encouragingly or shouted warnings to each of them as the hare or the monkey pushed each other near the edge of the platform and were in danger of falling over.

" Red-back ! Red-back ! stand your ground ! " called out the deer.

" Long-ears ! Long-ears ! be strong, be strong—don't let the monkey beat you ! " grunted the bear.

So the monkey and the hare, encouraged by their friends, tried their very hardest to beat each other.   The hare at last gained on the monkey.   The monkey seemed to trip up, and the hare giving him a good push sent him flying off the platform with a bound.

The poor monkey sat up rubbing his back, and his face

was very long as he screamed angrily, " Oh, oh ! how my back hurts—my back hurts me ! "

" Seeing the monkey in this plight on the ground, the deer holding his leaf on high said :

" This round is finished—the hare has won."

Kintaro then opened his luncheon box and taking out a rice-dumpling, gave it to the hare saying :

" Here is your prize, and you have earned it well ! "

Now the monkey got up looking very cross, and as they say in Japan " his stomach stood up," for he felt that he had not been fairly beaten. So he said to Kintaro and the others who were standing by :

" I have not been fairly beaten. My foot slipped and I tumbled. Please give me another chance and let the hare wrestle with me for another round."

Then Kintaro consenting, the hare and the monkey began to wrestle again. Now, as everyone knows, the monkey is a cunning animal by nature, and he made up his mind to get the best of the hare this time if it were possible. To do this, he thought that the best and surest way would be to get hold of the hare's long ear. This he soon managed to do. The hare was quite thrown off his guard by the pain of having his long ear pulled so hard, and the monkey seizing his opportunity at last, caught hold of one of the hare's legs and sent him sprawling in the middle of the daïs. The monkey was now the victor and received a rice-dumpling from Kintaro, which pleased him so much that he quite forgot his sore back.

The deer now came up and asked the hare if he felt ready for another round, and if so whether he would try a round with him, and the hare consenting, they both stood up to wrestle. The bear came forward as umpire.

The deer with long horns and the hare with long ears, it must have been an amusing sight to those who watched this queer match. Suddenly the deer went down on one of his knees, and the bear with the leaf on high declared him beaten. In this way, sometimes the one, sometimes the other, conquering, the little party amused themselves till they were tired.

At last Kintaro got up and said :

" This is enough for to-day. What a nice place we have found for wrestling ; let us come again to-morrow. Now, we will all go home. Come along ! " So saying, Kintaro led the way while the animals followed.

After walking some little distance they came out on the banks of a river flowing through a valley. Kintaro and his four furry friends stood and looked about for some means of crossing. Bridge there was none. The river rushed " don, don " on its way. All the animals looked serious, wondering how they could cross the stream and get home that evening.

Kintaro, however, said :

" Wait a moment. I will make a good bridge for you all in a few minutes."

The bear, the deer, the monkey and the hare looked at him to see what he would do now.

Kintaro went from one tree to another that grew along the river bank. At last he stopped in front of a very large tree that was growing at the water's edge. He took hold of the trunk and pulled it with all his might, once, twice, thrice ! At the third pull, so great was Kintaro's strength that the roots gave way, and " mèri, mèri " (crash, crash), over fell the tree, forming an excellent bridge across the stream.

" There," said Kintaro, " what do you think of my bridge ? It is quite safe, so follow me," and he stepped across first. The four animals followed. Never had they seen anyone so strong before, and they all exclaimed :

" How strong he is ! how strong he is ! "

While all this was going on by the river a woodcutter, who happened to be standing on a rock overlooking the stream, had seen all that passed beneath him. He watched with great surprise Kintaro and his animal companions. He rubbed his eyes to be sure that he was not dreaming when he saw this boy pull over a tree by the roots and throw it across the stream to form a bridge.

The woodcutter, for such he seemed to be by his dress, marvelled at all he saw, and said to himself :

" This is no ordinary child. Whose son can he be ? I will find out before this day is done."

He hastened after the strange party and crossed the bridge behind them. Kintaro knew nothing of all this, and little guessed that he was being followed. On reaching the other side of the river he and the animals separated, they to their lairs in the woods and he to his mother, who was waiting for him.

As soon as he entered the cottage, which stood like a matchbox in the heart of the pine-woods, he went to greet his mother, saying :

" Okkasan (mother), here I am ! "

" O, Kimbo ! " said his mother with a bright smile, glad to see her boy home safe after the long day. " How late you are to-day. I feared that something had happened to you. Where have you been all the time ? "

" I took my four friends, the bear, the deer, the monkey, and the hare, up into the hills, and there I made them try a wrestling match, to see which was the strongest. We all enjoyed the sport, and are going to the same place to-morrow to have another match."

" Now tell me who is the strongest of all ? " asked his mother, pretending not to know.

" Oh, mother," said Kintaro, " don't you know that I am the strongest ?   There was no need for me to wrestle with any of them."

" But next to you then, who is the strongest ? "

" The bear comes next to me in strength," answered Kintaro.

" And after the bear ? " asked his mother again.

" Next to the bear it is not easy to say which is the strongest, for the deer, the monkey, and the hare all seem to be as strong as each other," said Kintaro.

Suddenly Kintaro and his mother were startled by a voice from outside.

" Listen to me, little boy !   Next time you go, take this old man with you to the wrestling match.   He would like to join the sport too ! "

It was the old woodcutter who had followed Kintaro from the river.   He slipped off his clogs and entered the cottage. Yama-uba and her son were both taken by surprise.   They looked at the intruder wonderingly, and saw that he was someone they had never seen before.

" Who are you ? " they both exclaimed.

Then the woodcutter laughed and said :

" It does not matter who I am yet, but let us see who has the strongest arm—this boy or myself ? "

Then Kintaro, who had lived all his life in the forest, answered the old man without any ceremony, saying :

" We will have a try if you wish it, but you must not be angry whoever is beaten."

Then Kintaro and the woodcutter both put out their right arms and grasped each other's hands. For a long time Kintaro and the old man wrestled together in this way, each trying to bend the other's arm, but the old man was very strong, and the strange pair were evenly matched. At last the old man desisted, declaring it a drawn game.

" You are, indeed, a very strong child. There are few men who can boast of the strength of my right arm ! " said the woodcutter. " I saw you first on the banks of the river a few hours ago, when you pulled up that large tree to make a bridge across the torrent. Hardly able to believe what I saw I followed you home. Your strength of arm, which I have just tried, proves what I saw this afternoon. When you are full-grown you will surely be the strongest man in all Japan. It is a pity that you are hidden away in these wild mountains."

Then he turned to Kintaro's mother :

" And you, mother, have you no thought of taking your child to the Capital, and of teaching him to carry a sword as befits a *samurai* (a Japanese knight) ? "

" You are very kind to take so much interest in my son," replied the mother; " but he is as you see, wild and uneducated, and I fear it would be very difficult to do as you say.   Because of his great strength as an infant I hid him away in this unknown part of the country, for he hurt everyone that came

The Kind General gradually unfolded his Plan.

near him.   I have often wished that I could, one day, see my boy a knight wearing two swords, but as we have no influential friend to introduce us at the Capital, I fear my hope will never come true."

"You need not trouble yourself about that.   To tell you

the truth I am no woodcutter! I am one of the great generals of Japan. My name is Sadamitsu, and I am a vassal of the powerful Lord Minamoto-no-Raiko. He ordered me to go round the country and look for boys who give promise of remarkable strength, so that they may be trained as soldiers for his army. I thought that I could best do this by assuming the disguise of a woodcutter. By good fortune, I have thus unexpectedly come across your son. Now if you really wish him to be a *samurai* (a knight), I will take him and present him to the Lord Raiko as a candidate for his service. What do you say to this?"

As the kind general gradually unfolded his plan the mother's heart was filled with a great joy. She saw that here was a wonderful chance of the one wish of her life being fulfilled—that of seeing Kintaro a *samurai* before she died.

Bowing her head to the ground, she replied:

"I will then entrust my son to you if you really mean what you say."

Kintaro had all this time been sitting by his mother's side listening to what was said. When his mother finished speaking, he exclaimed:

"Oh, joy! joy! I am to go with the general and one day I shall be a *samurai!*"

Thus Kintaro's fate was settled, and the general decided to start for the Capital at once, taking Kintaro with him. It need hardly be said that Yama-uba was sad at parting with her boy, for he was all that was left to her. But she hid her grief with a strong face, as they say in Japan. She knew that it was for her boy's good that he should leave her now, and she must not discourage him just as he was setting out. Kintaro promised never to forget her, and said that as soon as he was a knight wearing two swords he would build her a home and take care of her in her old age.

All the animals, those he had tamed to serve him, the bear, the deer, the monkey, and the hare, as soon as they found out that he was going away, came to ask if they might attend him as usual. When they learned that he was going away for good they followed him to the foot of the mountain to see him off.

" Kimbo," said his mother, " mind and be a good boy."

" Mr. Kintaro," said the faithful animals, " we wish you good health on your travels."

Then they all climbed a tree to see the last of him, and from that height they watched him and his shadow gradually grow smaller and smaller, till he was lost to sight.

The general Sadamitsu went on his way rejoicing at having so unexpectedly found such a prodigy as Kintaro.

Having arrived at their destination the general took Kintaro at once to his Lord, Minamoto-no-Raiko, and told him all about Kintaro and how he had found the child. Lord Raiko was delighted with the story, and having commanded Kintaro to be brought to him, made him one of his vassals at once.

Lord Raiko's army was famous for its band called " The Four Braves." These warriors were chosen by himself from amongst the bravest and strongest of his soldiers, and the small and well-picked band was distinguished throughout the whole of Japan for the dauntless courage of its men.

When Kintaro grew up to be a man his master made him

the Chief of the Four Braves.   He was by far the strongest of
them all.   Soon after this event, news was brought to the city
that a cannibal monster had taken up his abode not far away

Lord Raiko ordered Kintaro to the Rescue.

and that people were stricken with fear.   Lord Raiko ordered
Kintaro to the rescue.   He immediately started off, delighted
at the prospect of trying his sword.

Surprising the monster in its den, he made short work

of cutting off its great head, which he carried back in triumph to his master.

Kintaro now rose to be the greatest hero of his country, and great was the power and honour and wealth that came to him.   He now kept his promise and built a comfortable home for his old mother, who lived happily with him in the Capital to the end of her days.

Is not this the story of a great hero ?

THE STORY OF PRINCESS HASE.

A Story of Old Japan.

Many, many years ago there lived in Nara, the ancient Capital of Japan, a wise State minister, by name Prince Toyonari Fujiwara. His wife was a noble, good, and beautiful woman called Princess Murasaki (Violet). They had been married by their respective families according to Japanese custom when very young, and had lived together happily ever since. They had, however, one cause for great sorrow, for as the years went by no child was born to them. This made them very unhappy, for they both longed to see a child of their own who would grow up to gladden their old age, carry on the family name, and keep up the ancestral rites when they were dead. The Prince and his lovely wife, after long consultation and much thought, determined to make a pilgrimage to the temple of Hase-no-Kwannon (Goddess of Mercy at Hase), for they believed, according to the beautiful tradition of their religion, that the Mother of Mercy, Kwannon, comes to answer the prayers of mortals in the form that they need the most. Surely after all these years of prayer she would come to them in the form of a beloved child in answer to their special pilgrimage, for that was the greatest need of their two lives. Everything else they had that this life could give them, but it was all as nothing because the cry of their hearts was unsatisfied.

So the Prince Toyonari and his wife went to the temple of Kwannon at Hase and stayed there for a long time, both daily offering incense and praying to Kwannon, the Heavenly Mother, to grant them the desire of their whole lives. And their prayer was answered.

A daughter was born at last to the Princess Murasaki, and great was the joy of her heart. On presenting the child to her husband they both decided to call her Hase-Hime, or the Princess of Hase, because she was the gift of the Kwannon at that place. They both reared her with great care and tenderness, and the child grew in strength and beauty.

When the little girl was five years old her mother fell dangerously ill and all the doctors and their medicines could not save her. A little before she breathed her last she called her daughter to her, and gently stroking her head, said:

"Hase-Hime, do you know that your mother cannot live any longer? Though I die, you must grow up a good girl. Do your best not to give trouble to your nurse or any other of your family. Perhaps your father will marry again and someone will fill my place as your mother. If so do not grieve for me, but look upon your father's second wife as your true mother, and be obedient and filial to both her and your father. Remember when you are grown up to be submissive to those who are your superiors, and to be kind to all those who are under you. Don't forget this. I die with the hope that you will grow up a model woman."

Hase-Hime listened in an attitude of respect while her

mother spoke, and promised to do all that she was told.
There is a proverb which says " As the soul is at three so it
is at one hundred," and so Hase-Hime grew up as her mother
had wished, a good and obedient little Princess, though she was
now too young to understand how great was the loss of her
mother.

Not long after the death of his first wife, Prince Toyonari

Hase-Hime listened in an Attitude of Respect.

married again, a lady of noble birth named Princess Terute.
Very different in character, alas ! to the good and wise Princess
Murasaki, this woman had a cruel, bad heart.   She did not love
her step-daughter at all, and was often very unkind to the little
motherless girl, saying to herself :

" This is not my child ! this is not my child ! "

But Hase-Hime bore every unkindness with patience, and
even waited upon her step-mother kindly and obeyed her in

every way and never gave any trouble, just as she had been trained by her own good mother, so that the Lady Terute had no cause for complaint against her.

The little Princess was very diligent, and her favourite studies were music and poetry. She would spend several hours practising every day, and her father had the most proficient of masters he could find to teach her the koto (Japanese harp), the art of writing letters and verse. When she was twelve years of age she could play so beautifully that she and her step-mother were summoned to the Palace to perform before the Emperor.

It was the Festival of the Cherry Flowers, and there were great festivities at the Court. The Emperor threw himself into the enjoyment of the season, and commanded that Princess Hase should perform before him on the koto, and that her mother Princess Terute should accompany her on the flute.

The Emperor sat on a raised daïs, before which was hung a curtain of finely-sliced bamboo and purple tassels, so that His Majesty might see all and not be seen, for no ordinary subject was allowed to look upon his sacred face.

Hase-Hime was a skilled musician though so young, and often astonished her masters by her wonderful memory and talent. On this momentous occasion she played well. But Princess Terute, her step-mother, who was a lazy woman and never took the trouble to practise daily, broke down in her accompaniment and had to request one of the Court ladies to take her place. This was a great disgrace, and she was furiously jealous to think that she had failed where her step-daughter succeeded ; and to make matters worse the Emperor

sent many beautiful gifts to the little Princess to reward her
for playing so well at the Palace.

There was also now another reason why Princess Terute
hated her step-daughter, for she had had the good fortune to
have a son born to her, and in her inmost heart she kept saying:

"If only Hase-Hime were not here, my son would have all
the love of his father."

And never having learned to control herself, she allowed
this wicked thought to grow into the awful desire of taking
her step-daughter's life.

So one day she secretly ordered some poison and poisoned
some sweet wine. This poisoned wine she put into a bottle.
Into another similar bottle she poured some good wine. It
was the occasion of the Boys' Festival on the fifth of May,
and Hase-Hime was playing with her little brother. All his toys
of warriors and heroes were spread out and she was telling him
wonderful stories about each of them. They were both enjoying
themselves and laughing merrily with their attendants when
his mother entered with the two bottles of wine and some
delicious cakes.

"You are both so good and happy," said the wicked
Princess Terute with a smile, "that I have brought you some
sweet wine as a reward—and here are some nice cakes for my
good children."

And she filled two cups from the different bottles.

Hase-Hime, never dreaming of the dreadful part her step-
mother was acting, took one of the cups of wine and gave to
her little step-brother the other that had been poured out
for him.

The wicked woman had carefully marked the poisoned
ttle, but on coming into the room she had grown nervous,
d pouring out the wine hurriedly had unconsciously given
e poisoned cup to her own child.   All this time she was
ixiously watching the little Princess, but to her amazement
） change whatever took place in the young girl's face.
uddenly the little boy screamed and threw himself on the
oor, doubled up with pain.   His mother flew to him, taking
he precaution to upset the two tiny jars of wine which she had
)rought into the room, and lifted him up.   The attendants rushed
or the doctor, but nothing could save the child—he died within
the hour in his mother's arms.   Doctors did not know much
in those ancient times, and it was thought that the wine had
disagreed with the boy, causing convulsions of which he died.

Thus was the wicked woman punished in losing her own
child when she had tried to do away with her step-daughter ;
but instead of blaming herself she began to hate Hase-Hime
more than ever in the bitterness and wretchedness of her own
heart, and she eagerly watched for an opportunity to do her
harm, which was, however, long in coming.

When Hase-Hime was thirteen years of age, she had already
become mentioned as a poetess of some merit.   This was an
accomplishment very much cultivated by the women of old
Japan and one held in high esteem.

It was the rainy season at Nara, and floods were reported
every day as doing damage in the neighbourhood.   The river
Tatsuta, which flowed through the Imperial Palace grounds,
was swollen to the top of its banks, and the roaring of the
torrents of water rushing along a narrow bed so disturbed the

Emperor's rest day and night, that a serious nervous disorder was the result. An Imperial Edict was sent forth to all the Buddhist temples commanding the priests to offer up continuous prayers to Heaven to stop the noise of the flood. But this was of no avail.

Then it was whispered in Court circles that the Princess Hase, the daughter of Prince Toyonari Fujiwara, second minister at Court, was the most gifted poetess of the day, though still so young, and her masters confirmed the report. Long ago, a beautiful and gifted maiden-poetess had moved Heaven by praying in verse, had brought down rain upon a land famished with drought—so said the ancient biographers of the poetess *Ono-no-Komachi*. If the Princess Hase were to write a poem and offer it in prayer, might it not stop the noise of the rushing river and remove the cause of the Imperial illness? What the Court said at last reached the ears of the Emperor himself, and he sent an order to the minister Prince Toyonari to this effect.

Great indeed was Hase-Hime's fear and astonishment when her father sent for her and told her what was required of her. Heavy, indeed, was the duty that was laid on her young shoulders—that of saving the Emperor's life by the merit of her verse.

At last the day came and her poem was finished. It was written on a leaflet of paper heavily flecked with gold-dust. With her father and attendants and some of the Court officials, she proceeded to the bank of the roaring torrent and raising up her heart to Heaven, she read the poem she had composed, aloud, lifting it heavenwards in her two hands.

Strange indeed it seemed to all those standing round. The waters ceased their roaring, and the river was quiet in direct answer to her prayer. After this the Emperor soon recovered his health.

His Majesty was highly pleased, and sent for her to the

Her Father sent for her, and told her what was Required of her.

Palace and rewarded her with the rank of *Chinjo*—that of Lieutenant-General—to distinguish her. From that time she was called Chinjo-hime, or the Lieutenant-General Princess, and respected and loved by all.

There was only one person who was not pleased at

Hase-Hime's success. That one was her step-mother. For ever brooding over the death of her own child whom she had killed when trying to poison her step-daughter, she had the mortification of seeing her rise to power and honour, marked by Imperial favour and the admiration of the whole Court. Her envy and jealousy burned in her heart like fire. Many were the lies she carried to her husband about Hase-Hime, but all to no purpose. He would listen to none of her tales, telling her sharply that she was quite mistaken.

At last the step-mother, seizing the opportunity of her husband's absence, ordered one of her old servants to take the innocent girl to the Hibari Mountains, the wildest part of the country, and to kill her there. She invented a dreadful story about the little Princess, saying that this was the only way to prevent disgrace falling upon the family—by killing her.

Katōda, her vassal, was bound to obey his mistress. Anyhow, he saw that it would be the wisest plan to pretend obedience in the absence of the girl's father, so he placed Hase-Hime in a palanquin and accompanied her to the most solitary place he could find in the wild district. The poor child knew there was no good in protesting to her unkind step-mother at being sent away in this strange manner, so she went as she was told.

But the old servant knew that the young Princess was quite innocent of all the things her step-mother had invented to him as reasons for her outrageous orders, and he determined to save her life. Unless he killed her, however, he could not return to his cruel task-mistress, so he decided to stay out in the wilderness. With the help of some peasants he soon built a little cottage, and having sent secretly for his wife to come, these two good old people did all in their power to take care of the now unfortunate Princess. She all the time trusted in her father, knowing that as soon as he returned home and found her absent, he would search for her.

Prince Toyonari, after some weeks, came home, and was told by his wife that his daughter Hase-Hime had done something wrong and had run away for fear of being punished. He was nearly ill with anxiety. Everyone in the house told the same story—that Hase-Hime had suddenly disappeared, none of them knew why or whither. For fear of scandal he kept the matter quiet and searched everywhere he could think of, but all to no purpose.

One day, trying to forget his terrible worry, he called all his men together and told them to make ready for a several days' hunt in the mountains. They were soon ready and mounted, waiting at the gate for their lord. He rode hard and fast to the district of the Hibari Mountains, a great company following him. He was soon far ahead of everyone, and at last found himself in a narrow picturesque valley.

Looking round and admiring the scenery, he noticed a tiny house on one of the hills quite near, and then he distinctly heard a beautiful clear voice reading aloud. Seized with curiosity as to who could be studying so diligently in such a lonely spot, he dismounted, and leaving his horse to his groom, he walked up the hillside and approached the cottage. As he drew nearer his surprise increased, for he could see that the reader was a beautiful girl. The cottage was wide open and she was sitting facing the view. Listening attentively, he heard her reading the Buddhist scriptures with great devotion.   More and more curious, he hurried on to the tiny gate and entered the little garden, and looking up beheld

Taken by Surprise, she could hardly realise that it was her Father.

his lost daughter Hase-Hime.   She was so intent on what she was saying that she neither heard nor saw her father till he spoke.

" Hase-Hime ! " he cried, " it is you, my Hase-Hime ! "

Taken by surprise, she could hardly realise that it was her

own dear father who was calling her, and for a moment she was utterly bereft of the power to speak or move.

" My father, my father! It is indeed you—oh, my father ! " was all she could say, and running to him she caught hold of his thick sleeve, and burying her face burst into a passion of tears.

Her father stroked her dark hair, asking her gently to tell him all that had happened, but she only wept on, and he wondered if he were not really dreaming.

Then the faithful old servant Katōda came out, and bowing himself to the ground before his master, poured out the long tale of wrong, telling him all that had happened, and how it was that he found his daughter in such a wild and desolate spot with only two old servants to take care of her.

The Prince's astonishment and indignation knew no bounds. He gave up the hunt at once and hurried home with his daughter. One of the company galloped ahead to inform the household of the glad news, and the step-mother hearing what had happened, and fearful of meeting her husband now that her wickedness was discovered, fled from the house and returned in disgrace to her father's roof, and nothing more was heard of her.

The old servant Katōda was rewarded with the highest promotion in his master's service, and lived happily to the end of his days, devoted to the little Princess, who never forgot that she owed her life to this faithful retainer. She was no longer troubled by an unkind step-mother, and her days passed happily and quietly with her father.

As Prince Toyonari had no son, he adopted a younger son

of one of the Court nobles to be his heir, and to marry his daughter Hase-Hime, and in a few years the marriage took place. Hase-Hime lived to a good old age, and all said that she was the wisest, most devout, and most beautiful mistress that had ever reigned in Prince Toyonari's ancient house. She had the joy of presenting her son, the future lord of the family, to her father just before he retired from active life.

To this day there is preserved a piece of needlework in one of the Buddhist temples of Kiōto. It is a beautiful piece of tapestry, with the figure of Buddha embroidered in the silky threads drawn from the stem of the lotus. This is said to have been the work of the hands of the good Princess Hase.

THE STORY OF THE MAN WHO DID NOT WISH TO DIE.

Long, long ago there lived a man called Sentaro. His surname meant " Millionaire," but although he was not so rich as all that, he was still very far removed from being poor. He had inherited a small fortune from his father and lived on this, spending his time carelessly, without any serious thoughts of work, till he was about thirty-two years of age.

One day, without any reason whatsoever, the thought of death and sickness came to him. The idea of falling ill or dying made him very wretched.

" I should like to live," he said to himself, " till I am five or six hundred years old at least, free from all sickness. The ordinary span of a man's life is very short."

He wondered whether it were possible, by living simply and frugally henceforth, to prolong his life as long as he wished.

He knew there were many stories in ancient history of emperors who had lived a thousand years, and there was a Princess of Yamato, who it was said, lived to the age of five hundred. This was the latest story of a very long life on record.

Sentaro had often heard the tale of the Chinese King named Shin-no-Shiko. He was one of the most able and powerful rulers in Chinese history. He built all the large palaces, and also the famous great wall of China. He had everything in the world he could wish for, but in spite of all his happiness, and the luxury and splendour of his Court, the wisdom of his councillors and the glory of his reign, he was miserable because he knew that one day he must die and leave it all.

When Shin-no-Shiko went to bed at night, when he rose in the morning, as he went through his day, the thought of death was always with him. He could not get away from it. Ah—if only he could find the "Elixir of Life," he would be happy.

The Emperor at last called a meeting of his courtiers and asked them all if they could not find for him the "Elixir of Life" of which he had so often read and heard.

One old courtier, Jofuku by name, said that far away across the seas there was a country called Horaizan, and that certain hermits lived there who possessed the secret of the "Elixir of Life." Whoever drank of this wonderful draught lived for ever.

The Emperor ordered Jofuku to set out for the land of Horaizan, to find the hermits, and to bring him back a phial of the magic elixir. He gave Jofuku one of his best junks, fitted it out for him, and loaded it with great quantities of treasures and precious stones for Jofuku to take as presents to the hermits.

Jofuku sailed for the land of Horaizan, but he never returned to the waiting Emperor; but ever since that time Mount Fuji has been said to be the fabled Horaizan and the home of hermits who had the secret of the elixir, and Jofuku has been worshipped as their patron god.

Now Sentaro determined to set out to find the hermits, and if he could, to become one, so that he might obtain the water of perpetual life. He remembered that as a child he had been told that not only did these hermits live on Mount Fuji, but that they were said to inhabit all the very high peaks.

So he left his old home to the care of his relatives, and started out on his quest. He travelled through all the mountainous regions of the land, climbing to the tops of the highest peaks, but never a hermit did he find.

At last, after wandering in an unknown region for many days, he met a hunter.

" Can you tell me," asked Sentaro, "where the hermits live who have the Elixir of Life ? "

" No," said the hunter; "I can't tell you where such hermits live, but there is a notorious robber living in these parts. It is said that he is chief of a band of two hundred followers."

This odd answer irritated Sentaro very much, and he thought how foolish it was to waste more time in looking for the hermits in this way, so he decided to go at once to the shrine of Jofuku, who is worshipped as the patron god of the hermits in the South of Japan.

Sentaro reached the shrine and prayed for seven days, entreating Jofuku to show him the way to a hermit who could give him what he wanted so much to find.

At midnight of the seventh day, as Sentaro knelt in the temple, the door of the innermost shrine flew open, and Jofuku appeared in a luminous cloud, and calling to Sentaro to come nearer, spoke thus :

"Your desire is a very selfish one and cannot be easily granted. You think that you would like to become a hermit so as to find the Elixir of Life. Do you know how hard a hermit's life is ? A hermit is only allowed to eat fruit and berries and the bark of pine trees ; a hermit must cut himself off from the world so that his heart may become as pure as gold and free from every earthly desire. Gradually after following these strict rules, the hermit ceases to feel hunger or cold or heat, and his body becomes so light that he can ride on a crane or a carp, and can walk on water without getting his feet wet.

"You, Sentaro, are fond of good living and of every comfort. You are not even like an ordinary man, for you are exceptionally idle, and more sensitive to heat and cold than most people. You would never be able to go barefoot or to wear only one thin dress in the winter time ! Do you think that you would ever have the patience or the endurance to live a hermit's life ?

"In answer to your prayer, however, I will help you in another way. I will send you to the country of Perpetual Life, where death never comes—where the people live for ever ! "

Saying this, Jofuku put into Sentaro's hand a little crane made of paper, telling him to sit on its back and it would carry him there.

Sentaro obeyed wonderingly. The crane grew large enough for him to ride on it with comfort. It then spread its wings, rose high in the air, and flew away over the mountains right out to sea.

Sentaro was at first quite frightened; but by degrees he grew accustomed to the swift flight through the air. On and

The Crane flew away, right out to Sea.

on they went for thousands of miles. The bird never stopped for rest or food, but as it was a paper bird it doubtless did not require any nourishment, and strange to say, neither did Sentaro.

After several days they reached an island. The crane flew some distance inland and then alighted.

As soon as Sentaro got down from the bird's back, the crane folded up of its own accord and flew into his pocket.

Now Sentaro began to look about him wonderingly, curious to see what the country of Perpetual Life was like. He walked first round about the country and then through the town. Everything was, of course, quite strange, and different from his own land. But both the land and the people seemed prosperous, so he decided that it would be good for him to stay there and took up lodgings at one of the hotels.

The proprietor was a kind man, and when Sentaro told him that he was a stranger and had come to live there, he promised to arrange everything that was necessary with the governor of the city concerning Sentaro's sojourn there. He even found a house for his guest, and in this way Sentaro obtained his great wish and became a resident in the country of Perpetual Life.

Within the memory of all the islanders no man had ever died there, and sickness was a thing unknown. Priests had come over from India and China and told them of a beautiful country called Paradise, where happiness and bliss and contentment fill all men's hearts, but its gates could only be reached by dying. This tradition was handed down for ages from generation to generation—but none knew exactly what death was except that it led to Paradise.

Quite unlike Sentaro and other ordinary people, instead of having a great dread of death, they all, both rich and poor, longed for it as something good and desirable. They were all tired of their long, long lives, and longed to go to the happy land of contentment called Paradise of which the priests had told them centuries ago.

All this Sentaro soon found out by talking to the islanders. He found himself, according to his ideas, in the land of *Topsyturvydom*. Everything was upside down. He had wished to escape from dying. He had come to the land of Perpetual Life with great relief and joy, only to find that the inhabitants themselves, doomed never to die, would consider it bliss to find death.

What he had hitherto considered poison these people ate as good food, and all the things to which he had been accustomed as food they rejected. Whenever any merchants from other countries arrived, the rich people rushed to them eager to buy poisons. These they swallowed eagerly hoping for death to come so that they might go to Paradise.

But what were deadly poisons in other lands were without effect in this strange place, and people who swallowed them with the hope of dying, only found that in a short time they felt better in health instead of worse.

Vainly they tried to imagine what death could be like. The wealthy would have given all their money and all their goods if they could but shorten their lives to two or three hundred years even. Without any change to live on for ever seemed to this people wearisome and sad.

In the chemist-shops there was a drug which was in constant demand, because after using it for a hundred years, it was supposed to turn the hair slightly grey and to bring about disorders of the stomach.

Sentaro was astonished to find that the poisonous globe-fish was served up in restaurants as a delectable dish, and hawkers in the streets went about selling sauces made of Spanish flies. He never saw anyone ill after eating these horrible things, nor did he ever see anyone with as much as a cold.

Sentaro was delighted. He said to himself that he would never grow tired of living, and that he considered it profane to wish for death. He was the only happy man on the island. For his part he wished to live thousands of years and to enjoy life. He set himself up in business, and for the present never even dreamed of going back to his native land.

As years went by, however, things did not go as smoothly as at first. He had heavy losses in business, and several times some affairs went wrong with his neighbours. This caused him great annoyance.

Time passed like the flight of an arrow for him, for he was busy from morning till night. Three hundred years went by in this monotonous way, and then at last he began to grow tired of life in this country, and he longed to see his own land and his old home. However long he lived here, life would always be the same, so was it not foolish and wearisome to stay on here for ever ?

Sentaro, in his wish to escape from the country of Perpetual Life, recollected Jofuku, who had helped him before when he was wishing to escape from death—and he prayed to the saint to bring him back to his own land again.

No sooner did he pray than the paper crane popped out of his pocket. Sentaro was amazed to see that it had remained undamaged after all these years. Once more the bird grew and grew till it was large enough for him to mount it. As he did so, the bird spread its wings and flew swiftly out across the sea in the direction of Japan.

Such was the wilfulness of the man's nature that he looked back and regretted all he had left behind. He tried to

He Screamed out to Jofuku to come and Rescue him.

stop the bird in vain. The crane held on its way for thousands of miles across the ocean.

Then a storm came on, and the wonderful paper crane got damp, crumpled up, and fell into the sea. Sentaro fell with it. Very much frightened at the thought of being drowned, he cried out loudly to Jofuku to save him. He looked round, but there was no ship in sight. He swallowed a quantity of sea-water, which only increased his miserable plight. While he was thus struggling to keep himself afloat, he saw a monstrous shark swimming towards him. As it came nearer it opened its huge mouth ready to devour him. Sentaro was all but paralysed with fear now that he felt his end so near, and screamed out as loudly as ever he could to Jofuku to come and rescue him.

Lo, and behold, Sentaro was awakened by his own screams, to find that during his long prayer he had fallen asleep before the shrine, and that all his extraordinary and frightful adventures had been only a wild dream. He was in a cold perspiration with fright, and utterly bewildered.

Suddenly a bright light came towards him, and in the light stood a messenger. The messenger held a book in his hand, and spoke to Sentaro :

" I am sent to you by Jofuku, who in answer to your prayer, has permitted you in a dream to see the land of Perpetual Life. But you grew weary of living there, and begged to be allowed to return to your native land so that you might die. Jofuku, so that he might try you, allowed you to drop into the sea, and then sent a shark to swallow you up. Your desire for death was not real, for even at that moment you cried out loudly and shouted for help.

" It is also vain for you to wish to become a hermit, or to find the Elixir of Life. These things are not for such as you—your life is not austere enough. It is best for you to go back to your paternal home, and to live a good and industrious life. Never neglect to keep the anniversaries of your ancestors, and make it your duty to provide for your children's future. Thus will you live to a good old age and be happy, but give up the vain desire to escape death, for no man can do that, and by this time you have surely found out that even when selfish desires are granted they do not bring happiness.

"In this book I give you there are many precepts good for you to know—if you study them, you will be guided in the way I have pointed out to you."

The angel disappeared as soon as he had finished speaking, and Sentaro took the lesson to heart. With the book in his hand he returned to his old home, and giving up all his old vain wishes, tried to live a good and useful life and to observe the lessons taught him in the book, and he and his house prospered henceforth.

THE BAMBOO-CUTTER AND THE MOON-CHILD.

Long, long ago, there lived an old bamboo woodcutter. He was very poor and sad also, for no child had Heaven sent to cheer his old age, and in his heart there was no hope of rest from work till he died and was laid in the quiet grave. Every morning he went forth into the woods and hills wherever the bamboo reared its lithe green plumes against the sky. When he had made his choice, he would cut down these feathers of the forest, and splitting them lengthwise, or cutting them into joints, would carry the bamboo wood home and make it into various articles for the household, and he and his old wife gained a small livelihood by selling them.

One morning as usual he had gone out to his work, and having found a nice clump of bamboos, had set to work to cut some of them down. Suddenly the green grove of bamboos was flooded with a bright soft light, as if the full moon had risen over the spot. Looking round in astonishment, he saw that the brilliance was streaming from one bamboo. The old man, full of wonder, dropped his axe and went towards the light. On nearer approach he saw that this soft splendour came from a hollow in the green bamboo stem, and still more wonderful to behold, in the midst of the brilliance stood a tiny human being, only three inches in height, and exquisitely beautiful in appearance.

He took the little Creature in his Hand.

"You must be sent to be my child, for I find you here among the bamboos where lies my daily work," said the old man, and taking the little creature in his hand he took it home to his wife to bring up. The tiny girl was so exceedingly beautiful and so small, that the old woman put her into a basket to safeguard her from the least possibility of being hurt in any way.

The old couple were now very happy, for it had been a life-long regret that they had no children of their own, and with joy they now expended all the love of their old age on the little child who had come to them in so marvellous a manner.

From this time on, the old man often found gold in the notches of the bamboos when he hewed them down and cut them up; not only gold, but precious stones also, so that by degrees he became rich. He built himself a fine house, and was no longer known as the poor bamboo woodcutter, but as a wealthy man.

Three months passed quickly away, and in that time the bamboo child had, wonderful to say, become a full-grown girl, so her foster-parents did up her hair and dressed her in beautiful *kimonos*. She was of such wondrous beauty that they placed her behind the screens like a princess, and allowed no one to see her, waiting upon her themselves. It seemed as if she were made of light, for the house was filled with a soft shining, so that even in the dark of night it was like daytime. Her presence seemed to have a benign influence on those there. Whenever the old man felt sad, he had only to look upon his foster-daughter and his sorrow vanished, and he became as happy as when he was a youth.

At last the day came for the naming of their new-found child, so the old couple called in a celebrated name-giver, and he gave her the name of Princess Moonlight, because her body gave forth so much soft bright light that she might have been a daughter of the Moon God.

For three days the festival was kept up with song and dance and music. All the friends and relations of the old couple were present, and great was their enjoyment of the festivities held to celebrate the naming of Princess Moonlight. Everyone who saw her declared that there never had been seen anyone so lovely ; all the beauties throughout the length and breadth of the land would grow pale beside her, so they said. The fame of the Princess's loveliness spread far and wide, and many were the suitors who desired to win her hand, or even so much as to see her.

Suitors from far and near posted themselves outside the house, and made little holes in the fence, in the hope of catching a glimpse of the Princess as she went from one room to the other along the verandah. They stayed there day and night, sacrificing even their sleep for a chance of seeing her, but all in vain. Then they approached the house, and tried to speak to the old man and his wife or some of the servants, but not even this was granted them.

Still, in spite of all this disappointment they stayed on day after day, and night after night, and counted it as nothing, so great was their desire to see the Princess.

At last, however, most of the men, seeing how hopeless their quest was, lost heart and hope both, and returned to their homes. All except five Knights, whose ardour and determination, instead of waning, seemed to wax greater with obstacles. These five men even went without their meals, and took snatches of whatever they could get brought to them, so that they might always stand outside the dwelling. They stood there in all weathers, in sunshine and in rain.

Sometimes they wrote letters to the Princess, but no answer was vouchsafed to them. Then when letters failed to draw any reply, they wrote poems to her telling her of the hopeless love which kept them from sleep, from food, from rest, and even from their homes. Still Princess Moonlight gave no sign of having received their verses.

In this hopeless state the winter passed. The snow and frost and the cold winds gradually gave place to the gentle warmth of spring. Then the summer came, and the sun burned white and scorching in the heavens above and on the earth beneath, and still these faithful Knights kept watch and waited. At the end of these long months they called out to the old bamboo-cutter and entreated him to have some mercy upon them and to show them the Princess, but he answered only that as he was not her real father he could not insist on her obeying him against her wishes.

The five Knights on receiving this stern answer returned to their several homes, and pondered over the best means of touching the proud Princess's heart, even so much as to grant them a hearing. They took their rosaries in hand and knelt before their household shrines, and burned precious incense, praying to Buddha to give them their hearts' desire. Thus several days passed, but even so they could not rest in their homes.

So again they set out for the bamboo-cutter's house. This time the old man came out to see them, and they asked him to let them know if it was the Princess's resolution never to see any man whatsoever, and they implored him to speak for them and to tell her the greatness of their love, and how long they had waited through the cold of winter and the heat of summer, sleepless and roofless through all weathers, without food and without rest, in the ardent hope of winning her, and they were willing to consider this long vigil as pleasure if she would but give them one chance of pleading their cause with her.

The old man lent a willing ear to their tale of love, for in his inmost heart he felt sorry for these faithful suitors and would have liked to see his lovely foster-daughter married to one of them. So he went in to Princess Moonlight and said reverently :

" Although you have always seemed to me to be a heavenly being, yet I have had the trouble of bringing you up as my own child and you have been glad of the protection of my roof. Will you refuse to do as I wish ? "

Then Princess Moonlight replied that there was nothing she would not do for him, that she honoured and loved him as her own father, and that as for herself she could not remember the time before she came to earth.

The old man listened with great joy as she spoke these dutiful words. Then he told her how anxious he was to see her safely and happily married before he died.

" I am an old man, over seventy years of age, and my end may come any time now. It is necessary and right that you should see these five suitors and choose one of them."

"Oh, why," said the Princess in distress, "must I do this? I have no wish to marry now."

"I found you," answered the old man, "many years ago, when you were a little creature three inches high, in the midst of a great white light. The light streamed from the bamboo in which you were hid and led me to you. So I have always thought that you were more than mortal woman. While I am alive it is right for you to remain as you are if you wish to do so, but some day I shall cease to be and who will take care of you then? Therefore I pray you to meet these five brave men one at a time and make up your mind to marry one of them!"

Then the Princess answered that she felt sure that she was not as beautiful as perhaps report made her out to be, and that even if she consented to marry any one of them, not really knowing her before, his heart might change afterwards. So as she did not feel sure of them, even though her father told her they were worthy Knights, she did not feel it wise to see them.

"All you say is very reasonable," said the old man, "but what kind of men will you consent to see? I do not call these five men who have waited on you for months, light-hearted. They have stood outside this house through the winter and the summer, often denying themselves food and sleep so that they may win you. What more can you demand?"

Then Princess Moonlight said she must make further trial of their love before she would grant their request to interview her. The five warriors were to prove their love by each bringing her from distant countries something that she desired to possess.

That same evening the suitors arrived and began to play their flutes in turn, and to sing their self-composed songs telling of their great and tireless love. The bamboo-cutter went out to them and offered them his sympathy for all they had endured and all the patience they had shown in their desire to win his foster-daughter. Then he gave them her message, that she would consent to marry whosoever was successful in bringing her what she wanted. This was to test them.

The five all accepted the trial, and thought it an excellent plan, for it would prevent jealousy between them.

Princess Moonlight then sent word to the First Knight that she requested him to bring her the stone bowl which had belonged to Buddha in India.

The Second Knight was asked to go to the Mountain of Horai, said to be situated in the Eastern Sea, and to bring her a branch of the wonderful tree that grew on its summit. The roots of this tree were of silver, the trunk of gold, and the branches bore as fruit white jewels.

The Third Knight was told to go to China and search for the fire-rat and to bring her its skin.

The Fourth Knight was told to search for the dragon that carried on its head the stone radiating five colours and to bring the stone to her.

The Fifth Knight was to find the swallow which carried a shell in its stomach and to bring the shell to her.

The old man thought these very hard tasks and hesitated to carry the messages, but the Princess would make no other conditions. So her commands were issued word for word to the five men who, when they heard what was required of them, were all disheartened and disgusted at what seemed to them the impossibility of the tasks given them and returned to their own homes in despair.

But after a time, when they thought of the Princess, the love in their hearts revived for her, and they resolved to make an attempt to get what she desired of them.

The First Knight sent word to the Princess that he was starting out that day on the quest of Buddha's bowl, and he hoped soon to bring it to her. But he had not the courage to go all the way to India, for in those days travelling was very difficult and full of danger, so he went to one of the temples in Kyoto and took a stone bowl from the altar there, paying the priest a large sum of money for it. He then wrapped it in a cloth of gold and, waiting quietly for three years, returned and carried it to the old man.

Princess Moonlight wondered that the Knight should have returned so soon. She took the bowl from its gold wrapping, expecting it to make the room full of light, but it did not shine at all, so she knew that it was a sham thing and not the true bowl of Buddha. She returned it at once and refused to see him. The Knight threw the bowl away and returned to his home in despair. He gave up now all hopes of ever winning the Princess.

The Second Knight told his parents that he needed change of air for his health, for he was ashamed to tell them that love for the Princess Moonlight was the real cause of his leaving them. He then left his home, at the same time sending word to the Princess that he was setting out for Mount Horai in the hope of getting her a branch of the gold and silver tree

which she so much wished to have. He only allowed his
servants to accompany him half-way, and then sent them back.
He reached the seashore and embarked on a small ship, and
after sailing away for three days he landed and employed several
carpenters to build him a house contrived in such a way that
no one could get access to it. He then shut himself up with
six skilled jewellers, and endeavoured to make such a gold and
silver branch as he thought would satisfy the Princess as
having come from the wonderful tree growing on Mount
Horai. Everyone whom he had asked declared that Mount
Horai belonged to the land of fable and not to fact.

When the branch was finished, he took his journey home
and tried to make himself look as if he were wearied and worn
out with travel. He put the jewelled branch into a lacquer
box and carried it to the bamboo-cutter, begging him to present
it to the Princess.

The old man was quite deceived by the travel-stained
appearance of the Knight, and thought that he had only just
returned from his long journey with the branch. So he tried
to persuade the Princess to consent to see the man. But she
remained silent and looked very sad. The old man began to
take out the branch and praised it as a wonderful treasure
to be found nowhere in the whole land. Then he spoke of
the Knight, how handsome and how brave he was to have
undertaken a journey to so remote a place as the Mount
of Horai.

Princess Moonlight took the branch in her hand and looked
at it carefully. She then told her foster-parent that she knew
it was impossible for the man to have obtained a branch from

the gold and silver tree growing on Mount Horai so quickly or so easily, and she was sorry to say she believed it artificial.

The old man then went out to the expectant Knight, who had now approached the house, and asked where he had found the branch.   Then the man did not scruple to make up a long story.

"Two years ago I took a ship and started in search of Mount Horai.   After going before the wind for some time I reached the far Eastern Sea.   Then a great storm arose and I was tossed about for many days, losing all count of the points of the compass, and finally we were blown ashore on an unknown island.   Here I found the place inhabited by demons who at one time threatened to kill and eat me.   However, I managed to make friends with these horrible creatures, and they helped me and my sailors to repair the boat, and I set sail again.   Our food gave out, and we suffered much from sickness on board.   At last, on the five-hundredth day from the day of starting, I saw far off on the horizon what looked like the peak of a mountain.   On nearer approach, this proved to be an island, in the centre of which rose a high mountain.   I landed, and after wandering about for two or three days, I saw a shining being coming towards me on the beach, holding in his hands a golden bowl.   I went up to him and asked him if I had, by good chance, found the island of Mount Horai, and he answered :

" ' Yes, this is Mount Horai ! '

"With much difficulty I climbed to the summit, where stood the golden tree growing with silver roots in the ground.   The wonders of that strange land are many, and if I began to tell you about them I could never stop. In spite of my wish to stay there long, on breaking off the branch I hurried back. With utmost speed it has taken me four hundred days to get back, and, as you see, my clothes are still damp from exposure on the long sea voyage. I have not even waited to change my raiment, so anxious was I to bring the branch to the Princess quickly."

Just at this moment the six jewellers, who had been employed on the making of the branch, but not yet paid by the Knight, arrived at the house and sent in a petition to the Princess to be paid for their labour. They said that they had worked for over a thousand days making the branch of gold, with its silver twigs and its jewelled fruit, that was now presented to her by the Knight, but as yet they had received nothing in payment. So this Knight's deception was thus found out, and the Princess, glad of an escape from one more importunate suitor, was only too pleased to send back the branch. She called in the workmen and had them paid liberally, and they went away happy. But on the way home they were overtaken by the disappointed man, who beat them till they were nearly dead, for letting out the secret, and they barely escaped with their lives. The Knight then returned home, raging in his heart; and in despair of ever winning the Princess gave up society and retired to a solitary life among the mountains.

Now the Third Knight had a friend in China, so he wrote to him to get the skin of the fire-rat. The virtue of any part of this animal was that no fire could harm it. He promised his friend any amount of money he liked to ask if only he could get him the desired article. As soon as the news came that the ship on which his friend had sailed home had come into port, he rode seven days on horseback to meet him. He handed his friend a large sum of money, and received the fire-rat's skin. When he reached home he put it carefully in a box and sent it in to the Princess while he waited outside for her answer.

The bamboo-cutter took the box from the Knight and, as usual, carried it in to her and tried to coax her to see the Knight at once, but Princess Moonlight refused, saying that she must first put the skin to test by putting it into the fire. If it were the real thing it would not burn. So she took off the crape wrapper and opened the box, and then threw the skin into the fire. The skin crackled and burnt up at once, and the Princess knew that this man also had not fulfilled his word. So the Third Knight failed also.

Now the Fourth Knight was no more enterprising than the rest. Instead of starting out on the quest of the dragon bearing on its head the five-colour-radiating jewel, he called all his servants together and gave them the order to seek for it far and wide in Japan and in China, and he strictly forbade any of them to return till they had found it.

His numerous retainers and servants started out in different directions, with no intention, however, of obeying what they considered an impossible order. They simply took a holiday, went to pleasant country places together, and grumbled at their master's unreasonableness.

The Knight meanwhile, thinking that his retainers could not fail to find the jewel, repaired to his house, and fitted it up beautifully for the reception of the Princess, he felt so sure of winning her.

One year passed away in weary waiting, and still his men did not return with the dragon-jewel. The Knight became desperate. He could wait no longer, so taking with him only two men, he hired a ship and commanded the captain to go in search of the dragon ; the captain and the sailors refused to undertake what they said was an absurd search, but the Knight compelled them at last to put out to sea.

When they had been but a few days out they encountered a great storm which lasted so long that, by the time its fury abated, the Knight had determined to give up the hunt of the dragon. They were at last blown on shore, for navigation was primitive in those days. Worn out with his travels and anxiety, the fourth suitor gave himself up to rest. He had caught a very heavy cold, and had to go to bed with a swollen face.

The governor of the place, hearing of his plight, sent messengers with a letter inviting him to his house. While he was there thinking over all his troubles, his love for the Princess turned to anger, and he blamed her for all the hardships he had undergone. He thought that it was quite probable she had wished to kill him so that she might be rid of him, and in order to carry out her wish had sent him upon his impossible quest.

At this point all the servants he had sent out to find the jewel came to see him, and were surprised to find praise instead of displeasure awaiting them. Their master told them that he was heartily sick of adventure, and said that he never intended to go near the Princess's house again in the future.

Like all the rest, the Fifth Knight failed in his quest—he could not find the swallow's shell.

By this time the fame of Princess Moonlight's beauty had reached the ears of the Emperor, and he sent one of the Court ladies to see if she were really as lovely as report said; if so he would summon her to the Palace and make her one of the ladies-in-waiting.

When the Court lady arrived, in spite of her father's entreaties, Princess Moonlight refused to see her. The Imperial messenger insisted, saying it was the Emperor's order. Then Princess Moonlight told the old man that if she were forced to go to the Palace in obedience to the Emperor's order, she would vanish from the earth.

When the Emperor was told of her persistence in refusing to obey his summons, and that if pressed to obey she would disappear altogether from sight, he determined to go and see her. So he planned to go on a hunting excursion in the neighbourhood of the bamboo-cutter's house, and see the Princess himself. He sent word to the old man of his intention, and he received consent to the scheme. The next day the Emperor set out with his retinue, which he soon managed to outride. He found the bamboo-cutter's house and dismounted. He then entered the house and went straight to where the Princess was sitting with her attendant maidens.

Never had he seen anyone so wonderfully beautiful, and he could not but look at her, for she was more lovely than any human being as she shone in her own soft radiance. When Princess Moonlight became aware that a stranger was looking at her she tried to escape from the room, but the Emperor caught her and begged her to listen to what he had to say. Her only answer was to hide her face in her sleeves.

The Emperor fell deeply in love with her, and begged her to come to the Court, where he would give her a position of honour and everything she could wish for. He was about to send for one of the Imperial palanquins to take her back with him at once, saying that her grace and beauty should adorn a Court and not be hidden in a bamboo-cutter's cottage.

But the Princess stopped him. She said that if she were forced to go to the Palace she would turn at once into a shadow, and even as she spoke she began to lose her form. Her figure faded from his sight while he looked.

The Emperor then promised to leave her free if only she would resume her former shape, which she did.

It was now time for him to return, for his retinue would be wondering what had happened to their Royal master when they missed him for so long. So he bade her good-bye, and left the house with a sad heart. Princess Moonlight was for him the most beautiful woman in the world ; all others were dark beside her, and he thought of her night and day. His Majesty now spent much of his time in writing poems, telling her of his love and devotion, and sent them to her, and though she refused to see him again she answered with many verses of her own composing, which told him gently and kindly that she could never marry anyone on this earth. These little songs always gave him pleasure.

At this time her foster-parents noticed that night after night the Princess would sit on her balcony and gaze for hours at the moon, in a spirit of the deepest dejection, ending always in a burst of tears. One night the old man found her thus weeping as if her heart were broken, and he besought her to tell him the reason of her sorrow.

With many tears she told him that he had guessed rightly when he supposed her not to belong to this world—that she had in truth come from the moon, and that her time on earth would soon be over. On the fifteenth day of that very month of August her friends from the moon would come to fetch her, and she would have to return. Her parents were both there, but having spent a lifetime on the earth she had forgotten them, and also the moon-world to which she belonged. It made her weep, she said, to think of leaving her kind foster-parents, and the home where she had been happy for so long.

When her attendants heard this they were very sad, and could not eat or drink for sadness at the thought that the Princess was so soon to leave them.

The Emperor, as soon as the news was carried to him, sent messengers to the house to find out if the report were true or not.

The old bamboo-cutter went out to meet the Imperial messengers. The last few days of sorrow had told upon the old man; he had aged greatly, and looked much more than his seventy years. Weeping bitterly, he told them that the report was only too true, but he intended, however, to make prisoners of the envoys from the moon, and to do all he could to prevent the Princess from being carried back.

The men returned and told His Majesty all that had passed. On the fifteenth day of that month the Emperor sent a guard of two thousand warriors to watch the house. One thousand stationed themselves on the roof, another thousand kept watch round all the entrances of the house. All were well trained archers, with bows and arrows. The bamboo-cutter and his wife hid Princess Moonlight in an inner room.

The old man gave orders that no one was to sleep that night, all in the house were to keep a strict watch, and be ready to protect the Princess. With these precautions, and the help of the Emperor's men-at-arms, he hoped to withstand the moon-messengers, but the Princess told him that all these measures to keep her would be useless, and that when her people came for her nothing whatever could prevent them from carrying out their purpose; even the Emperor's men would be powerless. Then she added with tears that she was very, very sorry to leave him and his wife, whom she had learnt to love as her parents; that if she could do as she liked she would stay with them in their old age, and try to make some return for all the love and kindness they had showered upon her during all her earthly life.

The night wore on! The yellow harvest moon rose high in the heavens, flooding the world asleep with her golden light. Silence reigned over the pine and the bamboo forests, and on the roof where the thousand men-at-arms waited.

Then the night grew grey towards the dawn and all hoped that the danger was over—that Princess Moonlight would not have to leave them after all. Then suddenly the watchers saw a cloud form round the moon—and while they looked this cloud began to roll earthwards. Nearer and nearer it came, and everyone saw with dismay that its course lay towards the house.

In a short time the sky was entirely obscured, till at last the cloud lay over the dwelling only ten feet off the ground. In the midst of the cloud there stood a flying chariot, and in the chariot a band of luminous beings. One amongst them who looked like a king and appeared to be the chief stepped out of the chariot and, poised in air, called to the old man to come out.

"The time has come," he said, "for Princess Moonlight to return to the moon from whence she came. She committed a grave fault, and as a punishment was sent to live down here for a time. We know what good care you have taken of the Princess, and we have rewarded you for this and have sent you wealth and prosperity. We put the gold in the bamboos for you to find."

"I have brought up this Princess for twenty years and never once has she done a wrong thing, therefore the lady you are seeking cannot be this one," said the old man. "I pray you to look elsewhere."

Then the messenger called aloud, saying :

"Princess Moonlight, come out from this lowly dwelling. Rest not here another moment."

At these words the screens of the Princess's room slid open of their own accord, revealing the Princess shining in her own radiance, bright and wonderful and full of beauty.

The messenger led her forth and placed her in the chariot. She looked back, and saw with pity the deep sorrow of the old man. She spoke to him many comforting words, and told him that it was not her will to leave him and that he must always think of her when looking at the moon.

The Screens slid open, revealing the Princess.

The bamboo-cutter implored to be allowed to accompany her, but this was not allowed. The Princess took off her embroidered outer garment and gave it to him as a keepsake.

One of the moon beings in the chariot held a wonderful coat of wings, another had a phial full of the Elixir of Life which was given the Princess to drink. She swallowed a little and was about to give the rest to the old man, but she was prevented from doing so.

The robe of wings was about to be put upon her shoulders, but she said :

"Wait a little. I must not forget my good friend the Emperor. I must write him once more to say good-bye while still in this human form."

In spite of the impatience of the messengers and charioteers she kept them waiting while she wrote. She placed the phial of the Elixir of Life with the letter, and, giving them to the old man, she asked him to deliver them to the Emperor.

Then the chariot began to roll heavenwards towards the moon, and as they all gazed with tearful eyes at the receding Princess, the dawn broke, and in the rosy light of day the moon-chariot and all in it were lost amongst the fleecy clouds that were now wafted across the sky on the wings of the morning wind.

Princess Moonlight's letter was carried to the Palace. His Majesty was afraid to touch the Elixir of Life, so he sent it with the letter to the top of the most sacred mountain in the land, Mount Fuji, and there the Royal emissaries burnt it on the summit at sunrise. So to this day people say there is smoke to be seen rising from the top of Mount Fuji to the clouds.

They all gazed with tearful eyes at the receding Princess.

THE MIRROR OF MATSUYAMA.

A STORY OF OLD JAPAN.

LONG years ago in old Japan there lived in the Province of Echigo, a very remote part of Japan even in these days, a man and his wife. When this story begins they had been married for some years and were blessed with one little daughter. She was the joy and pride of both their lives, and in her they stored an endless source of happiness for their old age.

What golden letter days in their memory were those that had marked her growing up from babyhood; the visit to the temple when she was just thirty days old, her proud mother carrying her, robed in ceremonial *kimono*, to be put under the patronage of the family's household god; then her first dolls' festival, when her parents gave her a set of dolls and their miniature belongings, to be added to as year succeeded year; and perhaps the most important occasion of all, on her third birthday, when her first *obi* (broad brocade sash) of scarlet and gold was tied round her small waist, a sign that she had crossed the threshold of girlhood and left infancy behind. Now that she was seven years of age, and had learned to talk and to wait upon her parents in those several little ways so dear to the hearts of fond parents, their cup of happiness seemed full. There could not be found in the whole of the Island Empire a happier little family.

The Wife gazed into the Shining Disc.

One day there was much excitement in the home, for the father had been suddenly summoned to the capital on business. In these days of railways and jinrickshas and other rapid modes of travelling, it is difficult to realise what such a journey as that from Matsuyama to Kyoto meant. The roads were rough and bad, and ordinary people had to walk every step of the way, whether the distance were one hundred or several hundred miles. Indeed, in those days it was as great an undertaking to go up to the capital as it is for a Japanese to make a voyage to Europe now.

So the wife was very anxious while she helped her husband get ready for the long journey, knowing what an arduous task lay before him. Vainly she wished that she could accompany him, but the distance was too great for the mother and child to go, and besides that, it was the wife's duty to take care of the home.

All was ready at last, and the husband stood in the porch with his little family round him.

" Do not be anxious, I will come back soon," said the man. " While I am away take care of everything, and especially of our little daughter."

" Yes, we shall be all right—but you—you must take care of yourself and delay not a day in coming back to us," said the wife, while the tears fell like rain from her eyes.

The little girl was the only one to smile, for she was ignorant of the sorrow of parting, and did not know that going to the capital was at all different from walking to the next village, which her father did very often. She ran to his side, and caught hold of his long sleeve to keep him a moment.

"Father, I will be very good while I am waiting for you to come back, so please bring me a present."

As the father turned to take a last look at his weeping wife and smiling, eager child, he felt as if someone were pulling him back by the hair, so hard was it for him to leave them

They watched him as he went down the Road.

behind, for they had never been separated before. But he knew that he must go, for the call was imperative. With a great effort he ceased to think, and resolutely turning away he went quickly down the little garden and out through the gate. His wife, catching up the child in her arms, ran as far as the gate, and watched him as he went down the road between the pines till he was lost in the haze of the distance and all she could see was his quaint peaked hat, and at last that vanished too.

" Now father has gone, you and I must take care of everything till he comes back," said the mother, as she made her way back to the house.

" Yes, I will be very good," said the child, nodding her head, " and when father comes home please tell him how good I have been, and then perhaps he will give me a present."

" Father is sure to bring you something that you want very much. I know, for I asked him to bring you a doll. You must think of father every day, and pray for a safe journey till he comes back."

" O, yes, when he comes home again how happy I shall be," said the child, clapping her hands, and her face growing bright with joy at the glad thought. It seemed to the mother as she looked at the child's face that her love for her grew deeper and deeper.

Then she set to work to make the winter clothes for the three of them. She set up her simple wooden spinning-wheel and spun the thread before she began to weave the stuffs. In the intervals of her work she directed the little girl's games and taught her to read the old stories of her country. Thus did the wife find consolation in work during the lonely days of her husband's absence. While the time was thus slipping quickly by in the quiet home, the husband finished his business and returned.

It would have been difficult for anyone who did not know the man well to recognise him. He had travelled day after day, exposed to all weathers, for about a month altogether, and was sunburnt to bronze, but his fond wife and child knew him at a glance, and flew to meet him from either side, each catching hold of one of his sleeves in their eager greeting.

"What I have brought you is called a Mirror."

Both the man and his wife rejoiced to find each other well. It seemed a very long time to all till—the mother and child helping—his straw sandals were untied, his large umbrella hat taken off, and he was again in their midst in the old familiar sitting-room that had been so empty while he was away.

As soon as they had sat down on the white mats, the father

opened a bamboo basket that he had brought in with him, and took out a beautiful doll and a lacquer box full of cakes.

"Here," he said to the little girl, "is a present for you.   It is a prize for taking care of mother and the house so well while I was away."

"Thank you," said the child, as she bowed her head to the ground, and then put out her hand just like a little maple leaf with its eager widespread fingers to take the doll and the box, both of which, coming from the capital, were prettier than anything she had ever seen.   No words can tell how delighted the little girl was—her face seemed as if it would melt with joy, and she had no eyes and no thought for anything else.

Again the husband dived into the basket, and brought out this time a square wooden box, carefully tied up with red and white string, and handing it to his wife, said :

"And this is for you."

The wife took the box, and opening it carefully took out a metal disc with a handle attached.   One side was bright and shining like a crystal, and the other was covered with raised figures of pine-trees and storks, which had been carved out of its smooth surface in lifelike reality.   Never had she seen such a thing in her life, for she had been born and bred in the rural province of Echigo.   She gazed into the shining disc, and looking up with surprise and wonder pictured on her face, she said :

"I see somebody looking at me in this round thing ! What is it that you have given me ?"

The husband laughed and said :

"Why, it is your own face that you see.   What I have

brought you is called a mirror, and whoever looks into its clear surface can see their own form reflected there. Although there are none to be found in this out of the way place, yet they have been in use in the capital from the most ancient times. There the mirror is considered a very necessary requisite for a woman to possess. There is an old proverb that ' As the sword is the soul of a samurai, so is the mirror the soul of a woman,' and according to popular tradition, a woman's mirror is an index to her own heart—if she keeps it bright and clear, so is her heart pure and good. It is also one of the treasures that form the insignia of the Emperor. So you must lay great store by your mirror, and use it carefully."

The wife listened to all her husband told her, and was pleased at learning so much that was new to her. She was still more pleased at the precious gift—his token of remembrance while he had been away.

" If the mirror represents my soul, I shall certainly treasure it as a valuable possession, and never will I use it carelessly." Saying so, she lifted it as high as her forehead, in grateful acknowledgment of the gift, and then shut it up in its box and put it away.

The wife saw that her husband was very tired, and set about serving the evening meal and making everything as comfortable as she could for him. It seemed to the little family as if they had not known what true happiness was before, so glad were they to be together again, and this evening the father had much to tell of his journey and of all he had seen at the great capital.

Time passed away in the peaceful home, and the parents

saw their fondest hopes realised as their daughter grew from childhood into a beautiful girl of sixteen. As a gem of priceless value is held in its proud owner's hand, so had they reared her with unceasing love and care : and now their pains were more than doubly rewarded. What a comfort she was to her mother as she went about the house taking her part in the housekeeping, and how proud her father was of her, for she daily reminded him of her mother when he had first married her.

But, alas! in this world nothing lasts for ever. Even the moon is not always perfect in shape, but loses its roundness with time, and flowers bloom and then fade. So at last the happiness of this family was broken up by a great sorrow. The good and gentle wife and mother was one day taken ill.

In the first days of her illness the father and daughter thought that it was only a cold, and were not particularly anxious. But the days went by and still the mother did not get better ; she only grew worse, and the doctor was puzzled, for in spite of all he did the poor woman grew weaker day by day. The father and daughter were stricken with grief, and day or night the girl never left her mother's side. But in spite of all their efforts the woman's life was not to be saved.

One day as the girl sat near her mother's bed, trying to hide with a cheery smile the gnawing trouble at her heart, the mother roused herself and taking her daughter's hand, gazed earnestly and lovingly into her eyes. Her breath was laboured and she spoke with difficulty:

" My daughter, I am sure that nothing can save me now.

When I am dead, promise me to take care of your dear father and to try to be a good and dutiful woman."

"Oh, mother," said the girl as the tears rushed to her eyes, "you must not say such things. All you have to do is

The Mother roused herself and took her Daughter's Hand.

to make haste and get well—that will bring the greatest happiness to father and myself."

"Yes, I know, and it is a comfort to me in my last days to know how greatly you long for me to get better, but it is not to be. Do not look so sorrowful, for it was so ordained in my previous state of existence that I should die in this life just at this time ; knowing this, I am quite resigned to my fate. And now I have something to give you whereby to remember me when I am gone."

Putting her hand out, she took from the side of the pillow a square wooden box tied up with a silken cord and tassels. Undoing this very carefully, she took out of the box the mirror that her husband had given her years ago.

"When you were still a little child your father went up to the capital and brought me back as a present this treasure ; it is called a mirror. This I give you before I die. If, after I have ceased to be in this life, you are lonely and long to see me sometimes, then take out this mirror and in the clear and shining surface you will always see me—so will you be able to meet with me often and tell me all your heart ; and though I shall not be able to speak, I shall understand and sympathise with you, whatever may happen to you in the future." With these words the dying woman handed the mirror to her daughter.

The mind of the good mother seemed to be now at rest, and sinking back without another word her spirit passed quietly away that day.

The bereaved father and daughter were wild with grief, and they abandoned themselves to their bitter sorrow. They felt it to be impossible to take leave of the loved woman who till now had filled their whole lives and to commit her body to the earth. But this frantic burst of grief passed, and then they took possession of their own hearts again, crushed though they were in resignation. In spite of this the daughter's life seemed to her desolate. Her love for her dead mother did not grow less with time, and so keen was her remembrance, that everything in daily life, even the falling of the rain and the blowing of the wind, reminded her of her mother's death and of all that they had loved and shared together. One day when her father was out, and she was fulfilling her household duties alone, her loneliness and sorrow seemed more than she could bear. She threw

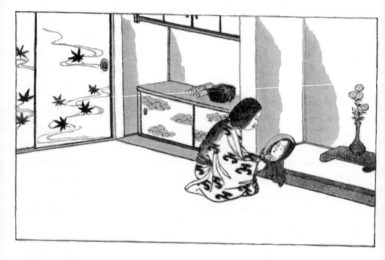

In the round Mirror before her she saw her Mother's Face.

herself down in her mother's room and wept as if her heart would break. Poor child, she longed just for one glimpse of the loved face, one sound of the voice calling her pet name, or for one moment's forgetfulness of the aching void in her heart. Suddenly she sat up. Her mother's last words had rung through her memory hitherto dulled by grief.

"Oh! my mother told me when she gave me the mirror as a parting gift, that whenever I looked into it I should be able to meet her—to see her. I had nearly forgotten her last words—how stupid I am; I will get the mirror now and see if it can possibly be true!"

She dried her eyes quickly, and going to the cupboard took out the box that contained the mirror, her heart beating with expectation as she lifted the mirror out and gazed into its smooth face. Behold, her mother's words were true! In the round mirror before her she saw her mother's face; but, oh, the joyful surprise! It was not her mother thin and wasted by illness, but the young and beautiful woman as she remembered her far back in the days of her own earliest childhood. It seemed to the girl that the face in the mirror must soon speak, almost that she heard the voice of her mother telling her again to grow up a good woman and a dutiful daughter, so earnestly did the eyes in the mirror look back into her own.

"It is certainly my mother's soul that I see. She knows how miserable I am without her and she has come to comfort me. Whenever I long to see her she will meet me here; how grateful I ought to be!"

And from this time the weight of sorrow was greatly lightened for her young heart. Every morning, to gather strength for the day's duties before her, and every evening, for consolation before she lay down to rest, did the young girl take out the mirror and gaze at the reflection which in the simplicity of her innocent heart she believed to be her mother's soul. Daily she grew in the likeness of her dead mother's character, and was gentle and kind to all, and a dutiful daughter to her father.

A year spent in mourning had thus passed away in the little household, when, by the advice of his relations, the man married again, and the daughter now found herself under the authority of a step-mother. It was a trying position; but her days spent in the recollection of her own beloved mother, and of trying to be what that mother would wish her to be, had made the young girl docile and patient, and she now determined to be filial and dutiful to her father's wife, in all respects. Everything went on apparently smoothly in the family for some time under the new *régime*; there were no winds or waves of discord to ruffle the surface of every day life, and the father was content.

But it is a woman's danger to be petty and mean, and step-mothers are proverbial all the world over, and this one's heart was not as her first smiles were. As the days and weeks grew into months, the step-mother began to treat the motherless girl unkindly and to try and come between the father and child.

Sometimes she went to her husband and complained of her step-daughter's behaviour, but the father knowing that this was to be expected, took no notice of her ill-natured complaints. Instead of lessening his affection for his daughter, as the woman desired, her grumblings only made him think of her the more. The woman soon saw that he began to show more concern for his lonely child than before. This did not please her at all, and she began to turn over in her mind how she could, by some means or other, drive her step-child out of the house. So crooked did the woman's heart become.

She watched the girl carefully, and one day peeping into her room in the early morning, she thought she discovered a grave enough sin of which to accuse the child to her father.

The woman herself was a little frightened too at what she had seen.

So she went at once to her husband, and wiping away some false tears she said in a sad voice :

" Please give me permission to leave you to-day."

The man was completely taken by surprise at the suddenness of her request, and wondered whatever was the matter.

" Do you find it so disagreeable," he asked, " in my house, that you can stay no longer ? "

" No ! no ! it has nothing to do with you—even in my dreams I have never thought that I wished to leave your side ; but if I go on living here I am in danger of losing my life, so I think it best for all concerned that you should allow me to go home ! "

And the woman began to weep afresh. Her husband, distressed to see her so unhappy, and thinking that he could not have heard aright, said :

" Tell me what you mean ! How is your life in danger here ? "

" I will tell you since you ask me. Your daughter dislikes me as her step-mother. For sometime past she has shut herself up in her room morning and evening, and looking in as I pass by, I am convinced that she has made an image of me and is trying to kill me by magic art, cursing me daily. It is not safe for me to stay here, such being the case ; indeed, indeed, I must go away, we cannot live under the same roof any more."

The husband listened to the dreadful tale, but he could not believe his gentle daughter guilty of such an evil act. He

knew that by popular superstition people believed that one
person could cause the gradual death of another by making an
image of the hated one and cursing it daily; but where had
his young daughter learned such knowledge?—the thing was
impossible.   Yet he remembered having noticed that his
daughter stayed much in her room of late and kept herself
away from everyone, even when visitors came to the house.
Putting this fact together with his wife's alarm, he thought
that there might be something to account for the strange
story.

His heart was torn between doubting his wife and trusting
his child, and he knew not what to do.   He decided to go at
once to his daughter and try to find out the truth.   Comforting
his wife and assuring her that her fears were groundless, he
glided quietly to his daughter's room.

The girl had for a long time past been very unhappy.   She
had tried by amiability and obedience to show her goodwill
and to mollify the new wife, and to break down that wall of
prejudice and misunderstanding that she knew generally stood
between step-parents and their step-children.   But she soon
found that her efforts were in vain.   The step-mother never
trusted her, and seemed to misinterpret all her actions, and the
poor child knew very well that she often carried unkind and
untrue tales to her father.   She could not help comparing her
present unhappy condition with the time when her own mother
was alive only a little more than a year ago—so great a
change in this short time!   Morning and evening she wept
over the remembrance.   Whenever she could she went to her
room, and sliding the screens to, took out the mirror and gazed,

as she thought, at her mother's face.   It was the only comfort that she had in these wretched days.

Her father found her occupied in this way.   Pushing aside the *fusama*, he saw her bending over something or other very intently.   Looking over her shoulder, to see who was entering her room, the girl was surprised to see her father, for he generally sent for her when he wished to speak to her.   She was also confused at being found looking at the mirror, for she had never told anyone of her mother's last promise, but had kept it as the sacred secret of her heart.   So before turning to her father she slipped the mirror into her long sleeve.   Her father noting her confusion, and her act of hiding something, said in a severe manner :

"Daughter, what are you doing here ?   And what is that that you have hidden in your sleeve ?"

The girl was frightened by her father's severity.   Never had he spoken to her in such a tone.   Her confusion changed to apprehension, her colour from scarlet to white.   She sat dumb and shamefaced, unable to reply.

Appearances were certainly against her ; the young girl looked guilty, and the father thinking that perhaps after all what his wife had told him was true, spoke angrily :

"Then, is it really true that you are daily cursing your step-mother and praying for her death ?   Have you forgotten what I told you, that although she is your step-mother you must be obedient and loyal to her ?   What evil spirit has taken possession of your heart that you should be so wicked ?   You have certainly changed, my daughter !   What has made you so disobedient and unfaithful ?"

And the father's eyes filled with sudden tears to think that he should have to upbraid his daughter in this way.

She on her part did not know what he meant, for she had never heard of the superstition that by praying over an image it is possible to cause the death of a hated person. But she saw that she must speak and clear herself somehow. She loved her father dearly, and could not bear the idea of his anger. She put out her hand on his knee deprecatingly:

"Father! father! do not say such dreadful things to me. I am still your obedient child. Indeed, I am. However stupid I may be, I should never be able to curse anyone who belonged to you, much less pray for the death of one you love. Surely someone has been telling you lies, and you are dazed, and you know not what you say—or some evil spirit has taken possession of *your* heart. As for me I do not know—no, not so much as a dew-drop, of the evil thing of which you accuse me."

But her father remembered that she had hidden something away when he first entered the room, and even this earnest protest did not satisfy him. He wished to clear up his doubts once for all.

"Then why are you always alone in your room these days? And tell me what is that that you have hidden in your sleeve— show it to me at once."

Then the daughter, though shy of confessing how she had cherished her mother's memory, saw that she must tell her father all in order to clear herself. So she slipped the mirror out from her long sleeve and laid it before him.

"This," she said, "is what you saw me looking at just now."

"Why," he said in great surprise, "this is the mirror that

I brought as a gift to your mother when I went up to the capital many years ago! And so you have kept it all this time? Now, why do you spend so much of your time before this mirror?"

Then she told him of her mother's last words, and of how she had promised to meet her child whenever she looked into the glass. But still the father could not understand the simplicity of his daughter's character in not knowing that what she saw reflected in the mirror was in reality her own face, and not that of her mother.

"What do you mean?" he asked. "I do not understand how you can meet the soul of your lost mother by looking in this mirror?"

"It is indeed true," said the girl; "and if you don't believe what I say, look for yourself," and she placed the mirror before her. There, looking back from the smooth metal disc, was her own sweet face. She pointed to the reflection seriously:

"Do you doubt me still?" she asked earnestly, looking up into his face.

With an exclamation of sudden understanding the father smote his two hands together.

"How stupid I am! At last I understand. Your face is as like your mother's as the two sides of a melon—thus you have looked at the reflection of your face all this time, thinking that you were brought face to face with your lost mother! You are truly a faithful child. It seems at first a stupid thing to have done, but it is not really so. It shows how deep has been your filial piety, and how innocent your heart. Living in constant remembrance of your lost mother has helped you to grow like her in character. How clever it was of her to tell you to do this. I admire and respect you, my daughter, and I am ashamed to think that for one instant I believed your suspicious step-mother's story and suspected you of evil, and came with the intention of scolding you severely, while all this time you have been so true and good. Before you I have no countenance left, and I beg you to forgive me."

And here the father wept. He thought of how lonely the poor girl must have been, and of all that she must have suffered under her step-mother's treatment. His daughter steadfastly keeping her faith and simplicity in the midst of such adverse circumstances—bearing all her troubles with so much patience and amiability—made him compare her to the lotus which rears its blossom of dazzling beauty out of the slime and mud of the moats and ponds, fitting emblem of a heart which keeps itself unsullied while passing through the world.

The step-mother, anxious to know what would happen, had all this while been standing outside the room. She had grown interested, and had gradually pushed the sliding screen back till she could see all that went on. At this moment she suddenly entered the room, and dropping to the mats, she bowed her head over her outspread hands before her step-daughter.

" I am ashamed! I am ashamed!" she exclaimed in broken tones. " I did not know what a filial child you were. Through no fault of yours, but with a step-mother's jealous heart, I have disliked you all the time. Hating you so much myself, it was but natural that I should think you reciprocated the feeling, and thus when I saw you retire so often to your room I followed you, and when I saw you gaze daily into the mirror for long intervals, I concluded that you had found out how I disliked you, and that you were out of revenge trying to take my life by magic art. As long as I live I shall never forget the wrong I have done you in so misjudging you, and in causing your father to suspect you. From this day I throw away my old and wicked heart, and in its place I put a new one, clean and full of repentance. I shall think of you as a child that I have borne myself. I shall love and cherish you with all my heart, and thus try to make up for all the unhappiness I have caused you. Therefore, please throw into the water all that has gone before, and give me, I beg of you, some of the filial love that you have hitherto given your own lost mother."

Thus did the unkind step-mother humble herself and ask forgiveness of the girl she had so wronged.

Such was the sweetness of the girl's disposition that she willingly forgave her step-mother, and never bore a moment's resentment or malice towards her afterwards. The father saw by his wife's face that she was truly sorry for the past, and was greatly relieved to see the terrible misunderstanding wiped out of remembrance by both the wrongdoer and the wronged.

From this time on, the three lived together as happily as fish in water. No such trouble ever darkened the home again, and the young girl gradually forgot that year of unhappiness in the tender love and care that her step-mother now bestowed on her. Her patience and goodness were rewarded at last.

THE GOBLIN OF ADACHIGAHARA.

Long, long ago there was a large plain called Adachigahara, in the province of Mutsu in Japan. This place was said to be haunted by a cannibal goblin who took the form of an old woman. From time to time many travellers disappeared and were never heard of more, and the old women round the charcoal braziers in the evenings, and the girls washing the household rice at the wells in the mornings, whispered dreadful stories of how the missing folk had been lured to the goblin's cottage and devoured, for the goblin lived only on human flesh. No one dared to venture near the haunted spot after sunset, and all those who could, avoided it in the daytime, and travellers were warned of the dreaded place.

One day as the sun was setting, a priest came to the plain. He was a belated traveller, and his robe showed that he was a Buddhist pilgrim walking from shrine to shrine to pray for some blessing or to crave for forgiveness of sins. He had apparently lost his way, and as it was late he met no one who could show him the road or warn him of the haunted spot.

He had walked the whole day and was now tired and hungry, and the evenings were chilly, for it was late autumn, and he began to be very anxious to find some house where he could obtain a night's lodging. He found himself lost in the midst of the large plain, and looked about in vain for some sign of human habitation.

At last, after wandering about for some hours, he saw a clump of trees in the distance, and through the trees he caught sight of the glimmer of a single ray of light.   He exclaimed with joy :

He pressed the Old Woman to let him Stay, but she seemed very Reluctant.

" Oh, surely that is some cottage where I can get a night's lodging ! "

Keeping the light before his eyes he dragged his weary, aching feet as quickly as he could towards the spot, and soon came to a miserable-looking little cottage.   As he drew near he saw that it was in a tumble-down condition, the bamboo fence was broken and weeds and grass pushed their way through the gaps. The paper screens which serve as windows and doors in Japan were full of holes, and the posts of the house were bent with age and seemed scarcely able to support the old thatched roof. The hut was open, and by the light of an old lantern an old woman sat industriously spinning.

The pilgrim called to her across the bamboo fence and said :

" O Baa San (old woman), good evening ! I am a traveller ! Please excuse me, but I have lost my way and do not know what to do, for I have nowhere to rest to-night. I beg you to be good enough to let me spend the night under your roof."

The old woman as soon as she heard herself spoken to stopped spinning, rose from her seat and approached the intruder.

" I am very sorry for you. You must indeed be distressed to have lost your way in such a lonely spot so late at night. Unfortunately I cannot put you up, for I have no bed to offer you, and no accommodation whatsoever for a guest in this poor place ! "

" Oh, that does not matter," said the priest; " all I want is a shelter under some roof for the night, and if you will be good enough just to let me lie on the kitchen floor I shall be grateful. I am too tired to walk further to-night, so I hope you will not refuse me, otherwise I shall have to sleep out on the cold plain." And in this way he pressed the old woman to let him stay.

She seemed very reluctant, but at last she said :

" Very well, I will let you stay here. I can offer you a very poor welcome only, but come in now and I will make a fire, for the night is cold."

The pilgrim was only too glad to do as he was told. He took off his sandals and entered the hut. The old woman then brought some sticks of wood and lit the fire, and bade her guest draw near and warm himself.

" You must be hungry after your long tramp," said the old woman. " I will go and cook some supper for you." She then went to the kitchen to cook some rice.

After the priest had finished his supper the old woman sat down by the fireplace, and they talked together for a long time. The pilgrim thought to himself that he had been very lucky to come across such a kind, hospitable old woman. At last the wood gave out, and as the fire died slowly down he began to shiver with cold just as he had done when he arrived.

" I see you are cold," said the old woman; " I will go out and gather some wood, for we have used it all. You must stay and take care of the house while I am gone."

" No, no," said the pilgrim, " let me go instead, for you are old, and I cannot think of letting you go out to get wood for me this cold night ! "

The old woman shook her head and said :

" You must stay quietly here, for you are my guest." Then she left him and went out.

In a minute she came back and said :

" You must sit where you are and not move, and whatever happens don't go near or look into the inner room. Now mind what I tell you ! "

" If you tell me not to go near the back room, of course I won't," said the priest, rather bewildered.

The old woman then went out again, and the priest was left

alone. The fire had died out, and the only light in the hut was that of a dim lantern. For the first time that night he began to feel that he was in a weird place, and the old woman's words, " Whatever you do don't peep into the back room," aroused his curiosity and his fear.

What hidden thing could be in that room that she did not wish him to see? For some time the remembrance of his promise to the old woman kept him still, but at last he could no longer resist his curiosity to peep into the forbidden place.

He got up and began to move slowly towards the back room. Then the thought that the old woman would be very angry with him if he disobeyed her made him come back to his place by the fireside.

As the minutes went slowly by and the old woman did not return, he began to feel more and more frightened, and to wonder what dreadful secret was in the room behind him. He must find out.

" She will not know that I have looked unless I tell her. I will just have a peep before she comes back," said the man to himself.

With these words he got up on his feet (for he had been sitting all this time in Japanese fashion with his feet under him) and stealthily crept towards the forbidden spot. With trembling hands he pushed back the sliding door and looked in. What he saw froze the blood in his veins. The room was full of dead men's bones and the walls were splashed and the floor was covered with human blood. In one corner skull upon skull rose to the ceiling, in another was a heap of arm bones, in another a heap of leg bones. The sickening smell made him faint. He fell backwards with horror, and for some time lay in a heap with fright on the floor, a pitiful sight. He trembled all over and his teeth chattered, and he could hardly crawl away from the dreadful spot.

What he saw froze the Blood in his Veins.

"How horrible!" he cried out. "What awful den have I come to in my travels? May Buddha help me or I am lost. Is it possible that that kind old woman is really the cannibal goblin? When she comes back she will show herself in her true character and eat me up at one mouthful!"

With these words his strength came back to him and,

snatching up his hat and staff, he rushed out of the house as
fast as his legs could carry him.   Out into the night he ran,
his one thought to get as far as he could from the goblin's

After him Rushed the Dreadful Old Hag.

haunt.   He had not gone far when he heard steps behind him
and a voice crying: " Stop ! stop ! "

He ran on, redoubling his speed, pretending not to hear.
As he ran he heard the steps behind him come nearer and
nearer, and at last he recognised the old woman's voice which
grew louder and louder as she came nearer.

" Stop ! stop, you wicked man, why did you look into the forbidden room ? "

The priest quite forgot how tired he was and his feet flew over the ground faster than ever. Fear gave him strength, for he knew that if the goblin caught him he would soon be one of her victims. With all his heart he repeated the prayer to Buddha :

" Namu Amida Butsu, Namu Amida Butsu."

And after him rushed the dreadful old hag, her hair flying in the wind, and her face changing with rage into the demon that she was. In her hand she carried a large blood-stained knife, and she still shrieked after him, " Stop ! stop ! "

At last, when the priest felt he could run no more, the dawn broke, and with the darkness of night the goblin vanished and he was safe. The priest now knew that he had met the Goblin of Adachigahara, the story of whom he had often heard but never believed to be true. He felt that he owed his wonderful escape to the protection of Buddha to whom he had prayed for help, so he took out his rosary and bowing his head as the sun rose he said his prayers and made his thanksgiving earnestly. He then set forward for another part of the country, only too glad to leave the haunted plain behind him.

THE SAGACIOUS MONKEY AND THE BOAR.

Long, long ago, there lived in the province of Shinshin in Japan, a travelling monkey-man, who earned his living by taking round a monkey and showing off the animal's tricks.

One evening the man came home in a very bad temper and told his wife to send for the butcher the next morning.

The wife was very bewildered and asked her husband :

" Why do you wish me to send for the butcher ? "

" It's no use taking that monkey round any longer, he's too old and forgets his tricks. I beat him with my stick all I know how, but he won't dance properly. I must now sell him to the butcher and make what money out of him I can. There is nothing else to be done."

The woman felt very sorry for the poor little animal, and pleaded for her husband to spare the monkey, but her pleading was all in vain, the man was determined to sell him to the butcher.

Now the monkey was in the next room and overheard every word of the conversation. He soon understood that he was to be killed, and he said to himself:

" Barbarous, indeed, is my master ! Here I have served him faithfully for years, and instead of allowing me to end my days comfortably and in peace, he is going to let me be cut up by the butcher, and my poor body is to be roasted and stewed

and eaten? Woe is me! What am I to do. Ah! a bright
thought has struck me! There is, I know, a wild boar living
in the forest near by. I have often heard tell of his wisdom.
Perhaps if I go to him and tell him the strait I am in he will
give me his counsel. I will go and try."

There was no time to lose. The monkey slipped out of the
house and ran as quickly as he could to the forest to find the

The Monkey began his Tale of Woe.

boar. The boar was at home, and the monkey began his tale
of woe at once.

"Good Mr. Boar, I have heard of your excellent wisdom.
I am in great trouble, you alone can help me. I have grown
old in the service of my master, and because I cannot dance
properly now he intends to sell me to the butcher. What do
you advise me to do? I know how clever you are!"

The boar was pleased at the flattery and determined to help the monkey. He thought for a little while and then said:

"Hasn't your master a baby?"

"Oh, yes," said the monkey, "he has one infant son."

"Doesn't it lie by the door in the morning when your mistress begins the work of the day? Well, I will come round early and when I see my opportunity I will seize the child and run off wi th it."

"What then?" said the monkey.

"Why the mother will be in a tremendous scare, and before your master and mistress know what to do, you must run after me and rescue the child and take it home safely to its parents, and you will see that when the butcher comes they won't have the heart to sell you."

The monkey thanked the boar many times and then went home. He did not sleep much that night, as you may imagine, for thinking of the morrow. His life depended on whether the boar's plan succeeded or not. He was the first up, waiting anxiously for what was to happen. It seemed to him a very long time before his master's wife began to move about and open the shutters to let in the light of day. Then all happened as the boar had planned. The mother placed her child near the porch as usual while she tidied up the house and got her breakfast ready.

The child was crooning happily in the morning sunlight, dabbing on the mats at the play of light and shadow. Suddenly there was a noise in the porch and a loud cry from the child. The mother ran out from the kitchen to the spot, only just in time to see the boar disappearing through the gate with her child in its clutch.   She flung out her hands with a loud cry of despair and rushed into the inner room where her husband was still sleeping soundly.

The Monkey was running after the Thief as fast as his Legs would carry him.

He sat up slowly and rubbed his eyes, and crossly demanded what his wife was making all that noise about.   By the time that the man was alive to what had happened, and they both got outside the gate, the boar had got well away, but they saw the monkey running after the thief as hard as his legs would carry him.

Both the man and wife were moved to admiration at the plucky conduct of the sagacious monkey, and their gratitude knew no bounds when the faithful monkey brought the child safely back to their arms.

" There ! " said the wife. " This is the animal you want to kill—if the monkey hadn't been here we should have lost our child for ever."

" You are right, wife, for once," said the man as he carried the child into the house. " You may send the butcher back when he comes, and now give us all a good breakfast and the monkey too."

When the butcher arrived he was sent away with an order for some boar's meat for the evening dinner, and the monkey was petted and lived the rest of his days in peace, nor did his master ever strike him again.

THE HAPPY HUNTER AND THE SKILFUL FISHER.

LONG, long ago Japan was governed by Hohodemi, the fourth Mikoto (or Augustness) in descent from the illustrious Amaterasu, the Sun Goddess. He was not only as handsome as his ancestress was beautiful, but he was also very strong and brave, and was famous for being the greatest hunter in the land. Because of his matchless skill as a hunter, he was called "Yama-sachi-hiko" or "The Happy Hunter of the Mountains."

His elder brother was a very skilful fisher, and as he far surpassed all rivals in fishing, he was named " Umi-sachi-hiko " or the " Skilful Fisher of the Sea." The brothers thus led happy lives, thoroughly enjoying their respective occupations, and the days passed quickly and pleasantly while each pursued his own way, the one hunting and the other fishing.

One day the Happy Hunter came to his brother, the Skilful Fisher, and said :

" Well, my brother, I see you go to the sea every day with your fishing rod in your hand, and when you return you come laden with fish. And as for me, it is my pleasure to take my bow and arrow and to hunt the wild animals up the mountains and down in the valleys. For a long time we have each followed our favourite occupation, so that now we must both be tired, you of your fishing and I of my hunting. Would it not be wise for us to make a change? Will you try hunting in the mountains and I will go and fish in the sea?"

The Skilful Fisher listened in silence to his brother, and for a moment was thoughtful, but at last he answered:

"O yes, why not? Your idea is not a bad one at all. Give me your bow and arrow and I will set out at once for the mountains and hunt for game."

So the matter was settled by this talk, and the two brothers each started out to try the other's occupation, little dreaming of all that would happen. It was very unwise of them, for the Happy Hunter knew nothing of fishing, and the Skilful Fisher, who was bad tempered, knew as much about hunting.

The Happy Hunter took his brother's much-prized fishing hook and rod and went down to the seashore and sat on the rocks. He baited his hook and then threw it into the sea clumsily. He sat and gazed at the little float bobbing up and down in the water, and longed for a good fish to come and be caught. Every time the buoy moved a little he pulled up his rod, but there was never a fish at the end of it, only the hook and the bait. If he had known how to fish properly, he would have been able to catch plenty of fish, but although he was the greatest hunter in the land he could not help being the most bungling fisher.

The whole day passed in this way, while he sat on the rocks holding the fishing rod and waiting in vain for his luck to turn. At last the day began to darken, and the evening came; still he had caught not a single fish. Drawing up his line for the last time before going home, he found that he had lost his hook without even knowing when he had dropped it.

The Happy Hunter in vain besought his Brother to Pardon him.

He now began to feel extremely anxious, for he knew that his brother would be angry at his having lost his hook for, it being his only one, he valued it above all other things. The Happy Hunter now set to work to look among the rocks and on the sand for the lost hook, and while he was searching to and fro, his brother, the Skilful Fisher, arrived on the scene. He had failed to find any game while hunting that day, and was not only in a bad temper, but looked fearfully cross. When he saw the Happy Hunter searching about on the shore he knew that something must have gone wrong, so he said at once :

" What are you doing, my brother ? "

The Happy Hunter went forward timidly, for he feared his brother's anger, and said :

" Oh, my brother, I have indeed done badly."

" What is the matter ?—what have you done ? " asked the elder brother impatiently.

" I have lost your precious fishing hook——"

While he was still speaking his brother stopped him, and cried out fiercely :

" Lost my hook ! It is just what I expected. For this reason, when you first proposed your plan of changing over our occupations I was really against it, but you seemed to wish it so much that I gave in and allowed you to do as you wished. The mistake of our trying unfamiliar tasks is soon seen ! And you have done badly. I will not return you your bow and arrow till you have found my hook. Look to it that you find it and return it to me quickly."

The Happy Hunter felt that he was to blame for all that had come to pass, and bore his brother's scornful scolding with

humility and patience. He hunted everywhere for the hook
most diligently, but it was nowhere to be found. He was at
last obliged to give up all hope of finding it. He then went
home, and in desperation broke his beloved sword into pieces
and made five hundred hooks out of it.

He took these to his angry brother and offered them to
him, asking his forgiveness, and begging him to accept them in
the place of the one he had lost for him. It was useless ; his
brother would not listen to him, much less grant his request.

The Happy Hunter then made another five hundred
hooks, and again took them to his brother, beseeching him
to pardon him.

"Though you make a million hooks," said the Skilful
Fisher, shaking his head, "they are of no use to me. I
cannot forgive you unless you bring me back my own hook."

Nothing would appease the anger of the Skilful Fisher, for
he had a bad disposition, and had always hated his brother
because of his virtues, and now with the excuse of the lost
fishing hook he planned to kill him and to usurp his place
as ruler of Japan. The Happy Hunter knew all this full well,
but he could say nothing, for being the younger he owed his
elder brother obedience ; so he returned to the seashore and
once more began to look for the missing hook. He was much
cast down, for he had lost all hope of ever finding his brother's
hook now. While he stood on the beach, lost in perplexity
and wondering what he had best do next, an old man
suddenly appeared carrying a stick in his hand. The Happy
Hunter afterwards remembered that he did not see from
whence the old man came, neither did he know how he was

there—he happened to look up and saw the old man coming towards him.

"You are Hohodemi, the Augustness, sometimes called the Happy Hunter, are you not?" asked the old man. "What are you doing alone in such a place?"

"Yes, I am he," answered the unhappy young man. "Unfortunately, while fishing I lost my brother's precious fishing hook. I have hunted this shore all over, but alas! I cannot find it, and I am very troubled, for my brother won't forgive me till I restore it to him. But who are you?"

"My name is Shiwozuchino Okina, and I live near by on this shore. I am sorry to hear what misfortune has befallen you. You must indeed be anxious. But if I tell you what I think, the hook is nowhere here—it is either at the bottom of the sea or in the body of some fish who has swallowed it, and for this reason, though you spend your whole life in looking for it here, you will never find it."

"Then what can I do?" asked the distressed man.

"You had better go down to Ryn Gu and tell Ryn Jin, the Dragon King of the Sea, what your trouble is and ask him to find the hook for you. I think that would be the best way."

"Your idea is a splendid one," said the Happy Hunter, "but I fear I cannot get to the Sea King's realm, for I have always heard that it is situated at the bottom of the sea."

"Oh, there will be no difficulty about your getting there," said the old man; "I can soon make something for you to ride on through the sea."

"Thank you," said the Happy Hunter, "I shall be very grateful to you if you will be so kind!"

The old man at once set to work, and soon made a basket and offered it to the Happy Hunter. He received it with joy, and taking it to the water, mounted it, and prepared to start. He bade good-bye to the kind old man who had helped him so much, and told him that he would certainly reward him as soon as he found his hook and could return to Japan without fear of his brother's anger. The old man pointed out the direction he must take, and told him how to reach the realm of Ryn Gu, and watched him ride out to sea on the basket, which resembled a small boat.

The Happy Hunter made all the haste he could, riding on the basket which had been given him by his friend. His queer boat seemed to go through the water of its own accord, and the distance was much shorter than he had expected, for in a few hours he caught sight of the gate and the roof of the Sea King's Palace. And what a large place it was, with its numberless sloping roofs and gables, its huge gateways, and its grey stone walls! He soon landed, and leaving his basket on the beach, he walked up to the large gateway. The pillars of the gate were made of beautiful red coral, and the gate itself was adorned with glittering gems of all kinds. Large *katsura* trees overshadowed it. Our hero had often heard of the wonders of the Sea King's Palace beneath the sea, but all the stories he had ever heard fell short of the reality which he now saw for the first time.

The Happy Hunter would have liked to enter the gate there and then, but he saw that it was fast closed, and also that there was no one about whom he could ask to open it for him, so he stopped to think what he should do. In the shade of the trees before the gate he noticed a well full of fresh spring water.   Surely someone would come out to draw water from the well some time, he thought.   Then he climbed into the tree overhanging the well, and seated himself to rest on one of the branches, and waited for what might happen.   Ere long he saw the huge gate swing open, and two beautiful women came out.   Now the Mikoto (Augustness) had always heard that Ryn Gu was the realm of the Dragon King under the Sea, and had naturally supposed that the place was inhabited by dragons and similar terrible creatures, so that when he saw these two lovely princesses, whose beauty would be rare even in the world from which he had just come, he was exceedingly surprised, and wondered what it could mean.

He said not a word, however, but silently gazed at them through the foliage of the trees, waiting to see what they would do.   He saw that in their hands they carried golden buckets.   Slowly and gracefully in their trailing garments they approached the well, standing in the shade of the *katsura* trees, and were about to draw water, all unknowing of the stranger who was watching them, for the Happy Hunter was quite hidden among the branches of the tree where he had posted himself.

As the two ladies leaned over the side of the well to let down their golden buckets, which they did every day in the year, they saw reflected in the deep still water the face of a handsome youth gazing at them from amidst the branches of the tree in whose shade they stood.   Never before had they seen the face of mortal man ; they were frightened, and drew back quickly with their golden buckets in their hands.   Their curiosity, however, soon gave them courage, and they glanced timidly upwards to see the cause of the unusual reflection, and then they beheld the Happy Hunter sitting in the tree looking down at them with surprise and admiration. They gazed at him face to face, but their tongues were still with wonder and they could not find a word to say to him.

When the Mikoto saw that he was discovered, he sprang down lightly from the tree and said :

" I am a traveller, and as I was very thirsty I came to the well in the hopes of quenching my thirst, but I could find no bucket with which to draw the water. So I climbed into the tree, much vexed, and waited for someone to come. Just at that moment, while I was thirstily and impatiently waiting, you noble ladies appeared, as if in answer to my great need. Therefore I pray you of your mercy give me some water to drink, for I am a thirsty traveller in a strange land."

His dignity and graciousness overruled their timidity, and bowing in silence they both once more approached the well, and letting down their golden buckets drew up some water and poured it into a jewelled cup and offered it to the stranger.

He received it from them with both hands, raising it to the height of his forehead in token of high respect and pleasure, and then drank the water quickly, for his thirst was great. When he had finished his long draught he set the cup down on the edge of the well, and drawing his short sword he cut off one of the strange curved jewels (*magatama*), a necklace of which hung round his neck and fell over his breast. He placed the jewel in the cup and returned it to them, and said, bowing deeply :

" This is a token of my thanks! "

The two ladies took the cup, and looking into it to see what he had put inside—for they did not yet know what it was —they gave a start of surprise, for there lay a beautiful gem at the bottom of the cup.

" No ordinary mortal would give away a jewel so freely. Will you not honour us by telling us who you are? " said the elder damsel.

" Certainly," said the Happy Hunter, " I am Hohodemi, the fourth Mikoto, also called in Japan, the Happy Hunter."

" Are you indeed Hohodemi, the grandson of Amaterasu, the Sun Goddess? " asked the damsel who had spoken first. " I am the eldest daughter of Ryn Jin, the King of the Sea, and my name is Princess Tayotama."

" And," said the younger maiden, who at last found her tongue, " I am her sister, the Princess Tamayori."

" Are you indeed the daughters of Ryn Jin, the King of the Sea? I cannot tell you how glad I am to meet you," said the Happy Hunter. And without waiting for them to reply he went on:

" The other day I went fishing with my brother's hook and dropped it, how, I am sure I can't tell. As my brother prizes his fishing hook above all his other possessions, this is the greatest calamity that could have befallen me. Unless I find it again I can never hope to win my brother's forgiveness, for he is very angry at what I have done. I have searched for it many, many times, but I cannot find it, therefore I am much troubled. While I was hunting for the hook, in great distress, I met a wise old man, and he told me that the best thing I could do was to come to Ryn Gu, and to Ryn Jin, the Dragon King of the Sea, and ask him to help me.   This kind old man also showed me how to come.   Now you know how it is I am here, and why.   I want to ask Ryn Jin if he knows where the lost hook is.   Will you be so kind as to take me to your father? And do you think he will see me?" asked the Happy Hunter anxiously.

Princess Tayotama listened to this long story, and then said:

" Not only is it easy for you to see my father, but he will be much pleased to meet you.   I am sure he will say that good fortune has befallen him, that so great and noble a man as you, the grandson of Amaterasu, should come down to the bottom of the sea."   And then turning to her younger sister, she said:

" Do you not think so, Tamayori?"

" Yes, indeed," answered the Princess Tamayori, in her sweet voice.   "As you say, we can know no greater honour than to welcome the Mikoto to our home."

" Then I ask you to be so kind as to lead the way," said the Happy Hunter.

" Condescend to enter, Mikoto (Augustness)," said both the sisters, and bowing low, they led him through the gate.

The younger Princess left her sister to take charge of the Happy Hunter, and going faster than they, she reached the Sea King's Palace first, and running quickly to her father's room, she told him of all that had happened to them at the gate, and that her sister was even now bringing the Augustness to him.   The Dragon King of the Sea was much surprised at the news, for it was but seldom, perhaps only once in several hundred years, that the Sea King's Palace was visited by mortals.

Ryn Jin at once clapped his hands and summoned all his courtiers and the servants of the Palace, and the chief fish of the sea together, and solemnly told them that the grandson of the Sun Goddess, Amaterasu, was coming to the Palace, and that they must be very ceremonious and polite in serving the august visitor. He then ordered them all to the entrance of the Palace to welcome the Happy Hunter.

Ryn Jin then dressed himself in his robes of ceremony, and went out to welcome him. In a few moments the Princess Tayotama and the Happy Hunter reached the entrance, and the Sea King and his wife bowed to the ground and thanked him for the honour he did them in coming to see them. The Sea King then led the Happy Hunter to the guest room, and placing him in the uppermost seat, he bowed respectfully before him, and said :

" I am Ryn Jin, the Dragon King of the Sea, and this is my wife. Condescend to remember us for ever ! "

" Are you indeed Ryn Jin, the King of the Sea, of whom I have so often heard ? " answered the Happy Hunter, saluting his host most ceremoniously. " I must apologise for all the trouble I am giving you by my unexpected visit." And he bowed again, and thanked the Sea King.

" You need not thank me," said Ryn Jin. " It is I who must thank you for coming. Although the Sea Palace is a poor place, as you see, I shall be highly honoured if you will make us a long visit."

There was much gladness between the Sea King and the Happy Hunter, and they sat and talked for a long time. At last the Sea King clapped his hands, and then a huge retinue of fishes appeared, all robed in ceremonial garments, and bearing in their fins various trays on which all kinds of sea delicacies were served. A great feast was now spread before the King and his Royal guest. All the fishes-in-waiting were chosen from amongst the finest fish in the sea, so you can imagine what a wonderful array of sea creatures it was that waited upon the Happy Hunter that day. All in the Palace tried to do their best to please him and to show him that he was a much honoured guest. During the long repast, which lasted for hours, Ryn Jin commanded his daughters to play some music, and the two Princesses came in and performed on the *koto* (the Japanese harp), and sang and danced in turns. The time passed so pleasantly that the Happy Hunter seemed to forget his trouble and why he had come at all to the Sea King's Realm, and he gave himself up to the enjoyment of this wonderful place, the land of fairy fishes ! Who has ever heard of such a marvellous place ? But the Mikoto soon remembered what had brought him to Ryn Gu, and said to his host :

" Perhaps your daughters have told you, King Ryn Jin, that I have come here to try and recover my brother's fishing hook, which I lost while fishing the other day. May I ask you to be so kind as to inquire of all your subjects if any of them have seen a fishing hook lost in the sea ? "

" Certainly," said the obliging Sea King, " I will immediately summon them all here and ask them."

As soon as he had issued his command, the octopus, the

cuttlefish, the bonito, the oxtail fish, the eel, the jelly fish, the shrimp, and the plaice, and many other fishes of all kinds came in and sat down before Ryn Jin their King, and arranged themselves and their fins in order. Then the Sea King said solemnly :

" Our visitor who is sitting before you all is the august grandson of Amaterasu. His name is Hohodemi, the fourth Augustness, and he is also called the Happy Hunter of the Mountains. While he was fishing the other day upon the shore of Japan, someone robbed him of his brother's fishing hook. He has come all this way down to the bottom of the sea to our Kingdom because he thought that one of you fishes may have taken the hook from him in mischievous play. If any of you have done so you must immediately return it, or if any of you know who the thief is you must at once tell us his name and where he is now."

All the fishes were taken by surprise when they heard these words, and could say nothing for some time. They sat looking at each other and at the Dragon King. At last the cuttlefish came forward and said :

" I think the *tai* (the red bream) must be the thief who has stolen the hook ! "

" Where is your proof ? " asked the King.

" Since yesterday evening the *tai* has not been able to eat anything, and he seems to be suffering from a bad throat ! For this reason I think the hook may be in his throat. You had better send for him at once ! "

All the fish agreed to this, and said :

" It is certainly strange that the *tai* is the only fish who has not obeyed your summons. Will you send for him and inquire into the matter. Then our innocence will be proved."

"Yes," said the Sea King, "it is strange that the *tai* has not come, for he ought to be the first to be here. Send for him at once!"

Without waiting for the King's order the cuttlefish had already started for the *tai's* dwelling, and he now returned, bringing the *tai* with him. He led him before the King.

The *tai* sat there looking frightened and ill. He certainly was in pain, for his usually red face was pale, and his eyes were nearly closed and looked but half their usual size.

"Answer, O *Tai!*" cried the Sea King, "why did you not come in answer to my summons to-day?"

"I have been ill since yesterday," answered the *tai;* "that is why I could not come."

"Don't say another word!" cried out Ryn Jin angrily. "Your illness is the punishment of the gods for stealing the Mikoto's hook."

"It is only too true!" said the *tai;* "the hook is still in my throat, and all my efforts to get it out have been useless. I can't eat, and I can scarcely breathe, and each moment I feel that it will choke me, and sometimes it gives me great pain. I had no intention of stealing the Mikoto's hook. I heedlessly snapped at the bait which I saw in the water, and the hook came off and stuck in my throat. So I hope you will pardon me."

The cuttlefish now came forward, and said to the King:

"What I said was right. You see the hook still sticks in the *tai's* throat. I hope to be able to pull it out in the

presence of the Mikoto, and then we can return it to him
safely!"

"O please make haste and pull it out!" cried the *tai*, piti-
fully, for he felt the pains in his throat coming on again; " I do
so want to return the hook to the Mikoto."

The Cuttlefish opened the *Tai's* Mouth.

"All right, *Tai San*," said his friend the cuttlefish, and then
opening the *tai's* mouth as wide as he could and putting one
of his feelers down the *tai's* throat, he quickly and easily drew
the hook out of the sufferer's large mouth.   He then washed it
and brought it to the King.

Ryn Jin took the hook from his subject, and then respectfully returned it to the Happy Hunter (the Mikoto or Augustness, the fishes called him), who was overjoyed at getting back his hook. He thanked Ryn Jin many times, his face beaming with gratitude, and said that he owed the happy ending of his quest to the Sea King's wise authority and kindness.

Ryn Jin now desired to punish the *tai*, but the Happy Hunter begged him not to do so; since his lost hook was thus happily recovered he did not wish to make more trouble for the poor *tai*. It was indeed the *tai* who had taken the hook, but he had already suffered enough for his fault, if fault it could be called. What had been done was done in heedlessness and not by intention. The Happy Hunter said he blamed himself; if he had understood how to fish properly he would never have lost his hook, and therefore all this trouble had been caused in the first place by his trying to do something which he did not know how to do. So he begged the Sea King to forgive his subject.

Who could resist the pleading of so wise and compassionate a judge? Ryn Jin forgave his subject at once at the request of his august guest. The *tai* was so glad that he shook his fins for joy, and he and all the other fish went out from the presence of their King, praising the virtues of the Happy Hunter.

Now that the hook was found the Happy Hunter had nothing to keep him in Ryn Gu, and he was anxious to get back to his own kingdom and to make peace with his angry brother, the Skilful Fisher; but the Sea King, who had learnt to love him and would fain have kept him as a son, begged him not to go so soon, but to make the Sea Palace his home as long as ever he liked. While the Happy Hunter was still hesitating, the two lovely Princesses, Tayotama and Tamayori, came, and with the sweetest of bows and voices joined with their father in pressing him to stay, so that without seeming ungracious he could not say them " Nay," and was obliged to stay on for some time.

Between the Sea Realm and the Earth there was no difference in the flight of time, and the Happy Hunter found that three years went fleeting quickly by in this delightful land. The years pass swiftly when anyone is truly happy. But though the wonders of that enchanted land seemed to be new every day, and though the Sea King's kindness seemed rather to increase than to grow less with time, the Happy Hunter grew more and more homesick as the days passed, and he could not repress a great anxiety to know what had happened to his home and his country and his brother while he had been away.

So at last he went to the Sea King and said :

" My stay with you here has been most happy and I am very grateful to you for all your kindness to me, but I govern Japan, and, delightful as this place is, I cannot absent myself for ever from my country. I must also return the fishing hook to my brother and ask his forgiveness for having deprived him of it for so long. I am indeed very sorry to part from you, but this time it cannot be helped. With your gracious permission, I will take my leave to day. I hope to make you another visit some day. Please give up the idea of my staying longer now."

King Ryn Jin was overcome with sorrow at the thought that he must lose his friend who had made a great diversion in the Palace of the Sea, and his tears fell fast as he answered :

" We are indeed very sorry to part with you, Mikoto, for we have enjoyed your stay with us very much. You have been a noble and honoured guest and we have heartily made you welcome. I quite understand that as you govern Japan you ought to be there and not here, and that it is vain for us to try and keep you longer with us, much as we would like to have you stay. I hope you will not forget us. Strange circumstances have brought us together and I trust the friendship thus begun between the Land and the Sea will last and grow stronger than it has ever been before."

When the Sea King had finished speaking he turned to his two daughters and bade them bring him the two Tide-Jewels of the Sea. The two Princesses bowed low, rose and glided out of the hall. In a few minutes they returned, each one carrying in her hands a flashing gem which filled the room with light. As the Happy Hunter looked at them he wondered what they could be. The Sea King took them from his daughters and said to his guest :

" These two valuable talismans we have inherited from our ancestors from time immemorial. We now give them to you as a parting gift in token of our great affection for you. These two gems are called the *Nanjiu* and the *Kanjiu*."

The Happy Hunter bowed low to the ground and said:

" I can never thank you enough for all your kindness to me. And now will you add one more favour to the rest and tell me what these jewels are and what I am to do with them ? "

" The *Nanjiu*," answered the Sea King, " is also called the Jewel of the Flood Tide, and whoever holds it in his possession can command the sea to roll in and to flood the land at any time that he wills.   The *Kanjiu* is also called the Jewel of the Ebbing Tide, and this gem controls the sea and the waves thereof, and will cause even a tidal wave to recede."

Then Ryn Jin showed his friend how to use the talismans one by one and handed them to him.   The Happy Hunter was very glad to have these two wonderful gems, the Jewel of the Flood Tide and the Jewel of the Ebbing Tide, to take back with him, for he felt that they would preserve him in case of danger from enemies at any time.   After thanking his kind host again and again, he prepared to depart.   The Sea King and the two Princesses, Tayotama and Tamayori, and all the inmates of the Palace, came out to say "Good-bye," and before the sound of the last farewell had died away the Happy Hunter passed out from under the great gateway, past the well of happy memory standing in the shade of the great *katsura* trees on his way to the beach.

Here he found, instead of the queer basket on which he had come to the Realm of Ryn Gu, a large crocodile waiting for him.   Never had he seen such a huge creature.   It measured eight fathoms in length from the tip of its tail to the end of its long mouth.   The Sea King had ordered the monster to carry the Happy Hunter back to Japan.   Like the wonderful basket which Shiwozuchino Okina had made, it could travel faster than any steamboat, and in this strange way, riding on the back of a crocodile, the Happy Hunter returned to his own land.

As soon as the crocodile landed him, the Happy Hunter hastened to tell the Skilful Fisher of his safe return. He then gave him back the fishing hook which had been found in the mouth of the *tai* and which had been the cause of so much trouble between them. He earnestly begged his brother's forgiveness, telling him all that had happened to him in the Sea King's Palace and what wonderful adventures had led to the finding of the hook.

Now the Skilful Fisher had used the lost hook as an excuse for driving his brother out of the country. When his brother had left him that day three years ago, and had not returned, he had been very glad in his evil heart and had at once usurped his brother's place as ruler of the land, and had become powerful and rich. Now in the midst of enjoying what did not belong to him, and hoping that his brother might never return to claim his rights, quite unexpectedly there stood the Happy Hunter before him.

The Skilful Fisher feigned forgiveness, for he could make no more excuses for sending his brother away again, but in his heart he was very angry and hated his brother more and more, till at last he could no longer bear the sight of him day after day, and planned and watched for an opportunity to kill him.

One day when the Happy Hunter was walking in the rice fields his brother followed him with a dagger. The Happy Hunter knew that his brother was following him to kill him, and he felt that now, in this hour of great danger, was the time to use the Jewels of the Flow and Ebb of the Tide and prove whether what the Sea King had told him was true or not.

So he took out the Jewel of the Flood Tide from the bosom
of his dress and raised it to his forehead.   Instantly over the

He took out the Jewel of the Flood Tide.

fields and over the farms the sea came rolling in wave upon
wave till it reached the spot where his brother was standing.
The Skilful Fisher stood amazed and terrified to see what was

happening. In another minute he was struggling in the water and calling on his brother to save him from drowning.

The Happy Hunter had a kind heart and could not bear the sight of his brother's distress. He at once put back the Jewel of the Flood Tide and took out the Jewel of the Ebb Tide. No sooner did he hold it up as high as his forehead than the sea ran back and back, and ere long the tossing rolling floods had vanished, and the farms and fields and dry land appeared as before.

The Skilful Fisher was very frightened at the peril of death in which he had stood, and was greatly impressed by the wonderful things he had seen his brother do. He learned now that he was making a fatal mistake to set himself against his brother, younger than he though he was, for he had now become so powerful that the sea would flow in and the tide ebb at his word of command. So he humbled himself before the Happy Hunter and asked him to forgive him all the wrong he had done him. The Skilful Fisher promised to restore his brother to his rights and also swore that though the Happy Hunter was the younger brother and owed him allegiance by right of birth, that he, the Skilful Fisher, would exalt him as his superior and bow before him as Lord of all Japan.

Then the Happy Hunter said that he would forgive his brother if he would throw into the receding tide all his evil ways. The Skilful Fisher promised and there was peace between the two brothers. From this time he kept his word and became a good man and a kind brother.

The Happy Hunter now ruled his Kingdom without being disturbed by family strife, and there was peace in Japan for a

long, long time.   Above all the treasures in his house he prized
the wonderful Jewels of the Flow and Ebb of the Tide which
had been given him by Ryn Jin, the Dragon King of the Sea.

    This is the congratulatory ending of the Happy Hunter and
the Skilful Fisher.

THE STORY OF THE OLD MAN WHO MADE WITHERED TREES TO FLOWER.

Long, long ago there lived an old man and his wife who supported themselves by cultivating a small plot of land. Their life had been a very happy and peaceful one save for one great sorrow, and this was that they had no child. Their only pet was a dog named Shiro, and on him they lavished all the affection of their old age. Indeed, they loved him so much that whenever they had anything nice to eat they denied themselves to give it to Shiro. Now Shiro means "white," and he was so called because of his colour. He was a real Japanese dog, and very like a small wolf in appearance.

The happiest hour of the day both for the old man and his dog was when the man returned from his work in the field, and having finished his frugal supper of rice and vegetables, would take what he had saved from the meal out to the little verandah that ran round the cottage. Sure enough, Shiro was waiting for his master and the evening tit-bit. Then the old man said " Chin, chin!" and Shiro sat up and begged, and his master gave him the food. Next door to this good old couple there lived another old man and his wife who were both wicked and cruel, and who hated their good neighbours and the dog Shiro with all their might. Whenever Shiro happened to look into their kitchen they at once kicked him or threw something at him, sometimes even wounding him.

One day Shiro was heard barking for a long time in the field at the back of his master's house. The old man, thinking that perhaps some birds were attacking the corn, hurried out

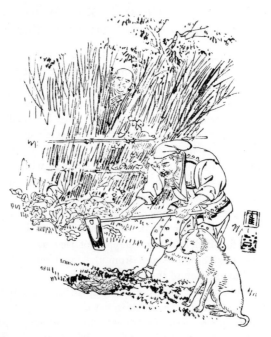

The deeper he Dug the more Gold Coins did the Old Man find.

to see what was the matter. As soon as Shiro saw his master he ran to meet him, wagging his tail, and, seizing the end of his *kimono*, dragged him under a large yenoki tree. Here he began to dig very industriously with his paws, yelping with joy all the time. The old man, unable to understand what it all meant, stood looking on in bewilderment. But Shiro went on barking and digging with all his might.

The thought that something might be hidden beneath the tree, and that the dog had scented it, at last struck the old man. He ran back to the house, fetched his spade and began to dig the ground at that spot. What was his astonishment when, after digging for some time, he came upon a heap of old and valuable coins, and the deeper he dug the more gold coins did he find. So intent was the old man on his work that he never saw the cross face of his neighbour peering at him through the bamboo hedge. At last all the gold coins lay shining on the ground. Shiro sat by erect with pride and looking fondly at his master as if to say, " You see, though only a dog, I can make some return for all the kindness you show me."

The old man ran in to call his wife, and together they carried home the treasure. Thus in one day did the poor old man become rich. His gratitude to the faithful dog knew no bounds, and he loved and petted him more than ever, if that were possible.

The cross old neighbour, attracted by Shiro's barking, had been an unseen and envious witness of the finding of the treasure. He began to think that he, too, would like to find a fortune. So a few days later he called at the old man's house and very ceremoniously asked permission to borrow Shiro for a short time.

Shiro's master thought this a strange request, because he knew quite well that not only did his neighbour not love his pet dog, but that he never lost an opportunity of striking and tormenting him whenever the dog crossed his path. But the good old man was too kind-hearted to refuse his neighbour, so he consented to lend the dog on the condition that he should be taken great care of.

The wicked old man returned to his home with an evil smile on his face, and told his wife how he had succeeded in his crafty intentions. He then took his spade and hastened to his own field, forcing the unwilling Shiro to follow him. As soon as he reached a yenoki tree, he said to the dog, threateningly:

"If there were gold coins under your master's tree, there must also be gold coins under my tree. You must find them for me! Where are they? Where? Where?"

And catching hold of Shiro's neck he held the dog's head to the ground, so that Shiro began to scratch and dig in order to free himself from the horrid old man's grasp.

The old man was very pleased when he saw the dog begin to scratch and dig, for he at once supposed that some gold coins lay buried under his tree as well as under his neighbour's, and that the dog had scented them as before; so pushing Shiro away he began to dig himself, but there was nothing to be found. As he went on digging a foul smell was noticeable, and he at last came upon a refuse heap.

The old man's disgust can be imagined. This soon gave place to anger. He had seen his neighbour's good fortune, and hoping for the same luck himself, he had borrowed the dog Shiro; and now, just as he seemed on the point of finding what he sought, only a horrid smelling refuse heap had rewarded

him for a morning's digging. Instead of blaming his own
greed for his disappointment, he blamed the poor dog. He
seized his spade, and with all his strength struck Shiro and
killed him on the spot. He then threw the dog's body into
the hole which he had dug in the hope of finding a treasure of
gold coins, and covered it over with the earth. Then he
returned to his house, telling no one, not even his wife, what
he had done.

After waiting several days, as the dog Shiro did not return,
his master began to grow anxious. Day after day went by,
and the good old man waited in vain. Then he went to his
neighbour and asked him to give him back his dog. Without
any shame or hesitation, the wicked neighbour answered that
he had killed Shiro because of his bad behaviour. At this
dreadful news Shiro's master wept many sad and bitter tears.
Great, indeed, was his woeful surprise, but he was too good
and gentle to reproach his bad neighbour. Learning that
Shiro was buried under the yenoki tree in the field, he asked
the old man to give him the tree, in remembrance of his poor
dog Shiro.

Even the cross old neighbour could not refuse such a
simple request, so he consented to give the old man the tree
under which Shiro lay buried. Shiro's master then cut the
tree down and carried it home. Out of the trunk he made a
mortar. In this his wife put some rice, and he began to pound
it with the intention of making a festival to the memory of his
dog Shiro.

A strange thing happened! His wife put the rice into the
mortar, and no sooner had he begun to pound it to make the

cakes, than it began to increase in quantity gradually till it was about five times the original amount, and the cakes were turned out of the mortar as if an invisible hand were at work.

When the old man and his wife saw this, they understood that it was a reward to them from Shiro for their faithful love to him. They tasted the cakes and found them nicer than any other food. So from this time they never troubled about food, for they lived upon the cakes with which the mortar never ceased to supply them.

The greedy neighbour, hearing of this new piece of good luck, was filled with envy as before, and called on the old man and asked leave to borrow the wonderful mortar for a short time, pretending that he, too, sorrowed for the death of Shiro, and wished to make cakes for a festival to the dog's memory.

The old man did not in the least wish to lend it to his cruel neighbour, but he was too kind to refuse. So the envious man carried home the mortar, but he never brought it back.

Several days passed, and Shiro's master waited in vain for the mortar, so he went to call on the borrower, and asked him to be good enough to return the mortar if he had finished with it. He found him sitting by a big fire made of pieces of wood. On the ground lay what looked very much like pieces of a broken mortar. In answer to the old man's inquiry, the wicked neighbour answered haughtily:

"Have you come to ask me for your mortar? I broke it to pieces, and now I am making a fire of the wood, for when I tried to pound cakes in it only some horrid smelling stuff came out."

The good old man said :

" I am very sorry for that. It is a great pity you did not ask me for the cakes if you wanted them. I would have given you as

The Withered Tree at once Burst into Full Bloom.

many as ever you wanted. Now please give me the ashes of the mortar, as I wish to keep them in remembrance of my dog."

The neighbour consented at once, and the old man carried home a basket full of ashes.

Not long after this the old man accidentally scattered some of the ashes made by the burning of the mortar on the trees of his garden. A wonderful thing happened!

It was late in autumn and all the trees had shed their leaves, but no sooner did the ashes touch their branches than the cherry trees, the plum trees, and all other blossoming shrubs burst into bloom, so that the old man's garden was suddenly transformed into a beautiful picture of spring. The old man's delight knew no bounds, and he carefully preserved the remaining ashes.

The story of the old man's garden spread far and wide, and people from far and near came to see the wonderful sight.

One day, soon after this, the old man heard some one knocking at his door, and going to the porch to see who it was he was surprised to see a Knight standing there. This Knight told him that he was a retainer of a great Daimio (Earl); that one of the favourite cherry trees in this nobleman's garden had withered, and that though everyone in his service had tried all manner of means to revive it, none took effect. The Knight was sore perplexed when he saw what great displeasure the loss of his favourite cherry tree caused the Daimio. At this point, fortunately, they had heard that there was a wonderful old man who could make withered trees to blossom, and that his Lord had sent him to ask the old man to come to him.

"And," added the Knight, "I shall be very much obliged if you will come at once."

The good old man was greatly surprised at what he

heard, but respectfully followed the Knight to the nobleman's Palace.

The Daimio, who had been impatiently awaiting the old man's coming, as soon as he saw him asked him at once :

" Are you the old man who can make withered trees flower even out of season ? "

The old man made an obeisance, and replied :

" I am that old man ! "

Then the Daimio said :

" You must make that dead cherry tree in my garden blossom again by means of your famous ashes. I shall look on."

Then they all went into the garden—the Daimio and his retainers and the ladies-in-waiting, who carried the Daimio's sword.

The old man now tucked up his *kimono* and made ready to climb the tree. Saying " Excuse me," he took the pot of ashes which he had brought with him, and began to climb the tree, everyone watching his movements with great interest.

At last he climbed to the spot where the tree divided into two great branches, and taking up his position here, the old man sat down and scattered the ashes right and left all over the branches and twigs.

Wonderful, indeed, was the result ! The withered tree at once burst into full bloom ! The Daimio was so transported with joy that he looked as if he would go mad. He rose to his feet and spread out his fan, calling the old man down from the tree. He himself gave the old man a wine cup filled with the best *saké*, and rewarded him with much silver and gold and many other precious things. The Daimio ordered that henceforth the old man should call himself by the name of *Hana-Saka-Jijii*, or "The Old Man who makes the Trees to

The Daimio ordered his Retainers to put the Impostor in Prison.

Blossom," and that henceforth all were to recognise him by this name, and he sent him home with great honour.

The wicked neighbour, as before, heard of the good old

man's fortune, and of all that had so auspiciously befallen him, and he could not suppress all the envy and jealousy that filled his heart.   He called to mind how he had failed in his attempt to find the gold coins, and then in making the magic cakes ; this time surely he must succeed if he imitated the old man, who made withered trees to flower simply by sprinkling ashes on them.   This would be the simplest task of all.

So he set to work and gathered together all the ashes which remained in the fireplace from the burning of the wonderful mortar.   Then he set out in the hope of finding some great man to employ him, calling out loudly as he went along :

" Here comes the wonderful man who can make withered trees blossom !   Here comes the old man who can make dead trees blossom ! "

The Daimio in his Palace heard this cry, and said :

" That must be the *Hana-Saka-Jijii* passing.   I have nothing to do to-day.   Let him try his art again; it will amuse me to look on."

So the retainers went out and brought in the impostor before their Lord.   The satisfaction of the false old man can now be imagined.

But the Daimio looking at him, thought it strange that he was not at all like the old man he had seen before, so he asked him :

" Are you the man whom I named *Hana-Saka-Jijii ?* "

And the envious neighbour answered with a lie :

" Yes, my Lord ! "

" That is strange ! " said the Daimio.   " I thought there was only one *Hana-Saka-Jijii* in the world !   Has he now some disciples ? "

" I am the true *Hana-Saka-Jijii*. The one who came to you before was only my disciple ! " replied the old man again.

" Then you must be more skilful than the other. Try what you can do and let me see ! "

The envious neighbour, with the Daimio and his Court following, then went into the garden, and approaching a dead tree, took out a handful of the ashes which he carried with him, and scattered them over the tree.

But not only did the tree not burst into flower, but not even a bud came forth. Thinking that he had not used enough ashes, the old man took handfuls and again sprinkled them over the withered tree. But all to no effect. After trying several times, the ashes were blown into the Daimio's eyes. This made him very angry, and he ordered his retainers to arrest the false *Hana-Saka-Jijii* at once and put him in prison for an impostor. From this imprisonment the wicked old man was never freed. Thus did he meet with punishment at last for all his evil doings.

The good old man, however, with the treasure of gold coins which Shiro had found for him, and with all the gold and the silver which the Daimio had showered on him, became a rich and prosperous man in his old age, and lived a long and happy life, beloved and respected by all.

THE JELLY FISH AND THE MONKEY.

LONG, long ago, in old Japan, the Kingdom of the Sea was governed by a wonderful King. He was called Rin Jin, or the Dragon King of the Sea. His power was immense, for he was the ruler of all sea creatures both great and small, and in his keeping were the Jewels of the Ebb and Flow of the Tide. The Jewel of the Ebbing Tide when thrown into the ocean caused the sea to recede from the land, and the Jewel of the Flowing Tide made the waves to rise mountains high and to flow in upon the shore like a tidal wave.

The Palace of Rin Jin was at the bottom of the sea, and was so beautiful that no one has ever seen anything like it even in dreams. The walls were of coral, the roof of jadestone and chrysoprase, and the floors were of the finest mother-of-pearl. But the Dragon King, in spite of his wide-spreading Kingdom, his beautiful Palace and all its wonders, and his power, which none disputed throughout the whole sea, was not at all happy, for he reigned alone. At last he thought that if he married he would not only be happier, but also more powerful. So he decided to take a wife. Calling all his fish retainers together, he chose several of them as ambassadors to go through the sea and seek for a young Dragon Princess who would be his bride.

At last they returned to the Palace bringing with them a lovely young dragon. Her scales were of a glittering green like the wings of summer beetles, her eyes threw out glances of fire, and she was dressed in gorgeous robes. All the jewels of the sea worked in with embroidery adorned them.

The King fell in love with her at once, and the wedding ceremony was celebrated with great splendour. Every living thing in the sea, from the great whales down to the little shrimps, came in shoals to offer their congratulations to the bride and bridegroom and to wish them a long and prosperous life. Never had there been such an assemblage or such gay festivities in the Fish-World before. The train of bearers who carried the bride's possessions to her new home seemed to reach across the waves from one end of the sea to the other. Each fish carried a phosphorescent lantern and was dressed in ceremonial robes, gleaming blue and pink and silver; and the waves as they rose and fell and broke that night seemed to be rolling masses of white and green fire, for the phosphorus shone with double brilliancy in honour of the event.

Now for a time the Dragon King and his bride lived very happily. They loved each other dearly, and the bridegroom day after day took delight in showing his bride all the wonders and treasures of his coral Palace, and she was never tired of wandering with him through its vast halls and gardens. Life seemed to them both like a long summer's day.

Two months passed in this happy way, and then the Dragon Queen fell ill and was obliged to stay in bed. The King was sorely troubled when he saw his precious bride so ill, and at once sent for the fish doctor to come and give her some medicine. He gave special orders to the servants to nurse her carefully and to wait upon her with diligence, but in spite of all the nurses' assiduous care and the medicine that the doctor prescribed, the young Queen showed no signs of recovery, but grew daily worse.

Then the Dragon King interviewed the doctor and blamed

The Dragon King Blamed the Doctor for not Curing the Queen.

him for not curing the Queen. The doctor was alarmed at Rin Jin's evident displeasure, and excused his want of skill by saying that although he knew the right kind of medicine to give the invalid, it was impossible to find it in the sea.

"Do you mean to tell me that you can't get the medicine here?" asked the Dragon King.

" It is just as you say ! " said the doctor.

" Tell me what it is you want for the Queen ? " demanded Rin Jin.

" I want the liver of a live monkey ! " answered the doctor.

" The liver of a live monkey ! Of course that will be most difficult to get," said the King.

" If we could only get that for the Queen, Her Majesty would soon recover," said the doctor.

"Very well, that decides it ; we *must* get it somehow or other. But where are we most likely to find a monkey ? " asked the King.

Then the doctor told the Dragon King that some distance to the south there was a Monkey Island where a great many monkeys lived.

" If only you could capture one of those monkeys ? " said the doctor.

" How can any of my people capture a monkey ? " said the Dragon King, greatly puzzled. " The monkeys live on dry land, while we live in the water; and out of our element we are quite powerless ! I don't see what we can do ! "

" That has been my difficulty too," said the doctor. " But amongst your innumerable servants, you surely can find one who can go on shore for that express purpose ! "

" Something must be done," said the King, and calling his chief steward he consulted him on the matter.

The chief steward thought for some time, and then, as if struck by a sudden thought, said joyfully :

" I know what we must do ! There is the *kurage* (jelly fish). He is certainly ugly to look at, but he is proud of being able to walk on land with his four legs like a tortoise. Let us send him to the Island of Monkeys to catch one."

The jelly fish was then summoned to the King's presence, and was told by His Majesty what was required of him.

The jelly fish, on being told of the unexpected mission which was to be entrusted to him, looked very troubled, and said that he had never been to the island in question, and as he had never had any experience in catching monkeys he was afraid that he would not be able to get one.

"Well," said the chief steward, "if you depend on your strength or dexterity you will never catch a monkey. The only way is to play a trick on one!"

"How can I play a trick on a monkey? I don't know how to do it," said the perplexed jelly fish.

"This is what you must do," said the wily chief steward. "When you approach the Island of Monkeys and meet some of them, you must try to get very friendly with one. Tell him that you are a servant of the Dragon King, and invite him to come and visit you and see the Dragon King's Palace. Try and describe to him as vividly as you can the grandeur of the Palace and the wonders of the sea so as to arouse his curiosity and make him long to see it all!"

"But how am I to get the monkey here? You know monkeys don't swim!" said the reluctant jelly fish.

"You must carry him on your back. What is the use of your shell if you can't do that!" said the chief steward.

"Won't he be very heavy?" queried *kurage* again.

"You mustn't mind that, for you are working for the Dragon King!" replied the chief steward.

" I will do my best then," said the jelly fish, and he swam away from the Palace and started off towards the Monkey Island. Swimming swiftly he reached his destination in a few hours, and was landed by a convenient wave upon the shore. On looking round he saw not far away a big pine-tree with drooping branches and on one of those branches was just what he was looking for—a live monkey.

" I'm in luck!" thought the jelly fish. " Now I must flatter the creature and try to entice him to come back with me to the Palace, and my part will be done ! "

So the jelly fish slowly walked towards the pine-tree. In those ancient days the jelly fish had four legs and a hard shell like a tortoise. When he got to the pine-tree he raised his voice and said :

" How do you do, Mr. Monkey ?   Isn't it a lovely day ? "

" A very fine day," answered the monkey from the tree. " I have never seen you in this part of the world before. Where have you come from and what is your name ? "

" My name is *kurage* or jelly fish. I am one of the servants of the Dragon King. I have heard so much of your beautiful island that I have come on purpose to see it," answered the jelly fish.

" I am very glad to see you," said the monkey.

" By-the-bye," said the jelly fish, " have you ever seen the Palace of the Dragon King of the Sea where I live ? "

" I have often heard of it, but I have never seen it ! " answered the monkey.

" Then you ought most surely to come. It is a great pity for you to go through life without seeing it. The beauty of the Palace is beyond all description—it is certainly to my mind the most lovely place in the world," said the jelly fish.

"Is it so beautiful as all that?" asked the monkey in astonishment.

Then the jelly fish saw his chance, and went on describing to the best of his ability the beauty and grandeur of the Sea King's Palace, and the wonders of the garden with its curious trees of white, pink and red coral, and the still more curious fruits like great jewels hanging on the branches. The monkey grew more and more interested, and as he listened he came down the tree step by step so as not to lose a word of the wonderful story.

"I have got him at last!" thought the jelly fish, but aloud he said:

"Mr. Monkey, I must now go back. As you have never seen the Palace of the Dragon King, won't you avail yourself of this splendid opportunity by coming with me? I shall then be able to act as guide and show you all the sights of the sea, which will be even more wonderful to you —a land-lubber."

"I should love to go," said the monkey, "but how am I to cross the water? I can't swim, as you surely know!"

"There is no difficulty about that. I can carry you on my back."

"That will be troubling you too much," said the monkey.

"I can do it quite easily. I am stronger than I look, so you needn't hesitate," said the jelly fish, and taking the monkey on his back he stepped into the sea.

"Keep very still, Mr. Monkey," said the jelly fish. "You

mustn't fall into the sea; I am responsible for your safe arrival at the King's Palace."

"Please don't go so fast, or I am sure I shall fall off," said the monkey.

Thus they went along, the jelly fish skimming through the

"Please don't go so fast, or I am sure I shall fall off," said the Monkey.

waves with the monkey sitting on his back. When they were about half-way, the jelly fish, who knew very little of anatomy, began to wonder if the monkey had his liver with him or not!

"Mr. Monkey, tell me, have you such a thing as a liver with you?"

The monkey was very much surprised at this queer question, and asked what the jelly fish wanted with a liver.

" That is the most important thing of all," said the stupid jelly fish, " so as soon as I recollected it, I asked you if you had yours with you ? "

" Why is my liver so important to you ? " asked the monkey.

" Oh ! you will learn the reason later," said the jelly fish.

The monkey grew more and more curious and suspicious, and urged the jelly fish to tell him for what his liver was wanted, and ended up by appealing to his hearer's feelings by saying that he was very troubled at what he had been told.

Then the jelly fish, seeing how anxious the monkey looked, was sorry for him, and told him everything. How the Dragon Queen had fallen ill, and how the doctor had said that only the liver of a live monkey would cure her, and how the Dragon King had sent him to find one.

" Now I have done as I was told, and as soon as we arrive at the Palace the doctor will want your liver, so I feel sorry for you ! " said the silly jelly fish.

The poor monkey was horrified when he learnt all this, and very angry at the trick played upon him. He trembled with fear at the thought of what was in store for him.

But the monkey was a clever animal, and he thought it the wisest plan not to show any sign of the fear he felt, so he tried to calm himself and to think of some way by which he might escape.

" The doctor means to cut me open and then take my liver out ! Why I shall die ! " thought the monkey. At last a bright thought struck him, so he said quite cheerfully to the jelly fish :

" What a pity it was, Mr. Jelly Fish, that you did not speak of this before we left the island ! "

" If I had told you why I wanted you to accompany me you would certainly have refused to come," answered the jelly fish.

" You are quite mistaken," said the monkey. " Monkeys can very well spare a liver or two, especially when it is wanted for the Dragon Queen of the Sea. If I had only guessed of what you were in need, I should have presented you with one without waiting to be asked. I have several livers. But the greatest pity is, that as you did not speak in time, I have left all my livers hanging on the pine-tree."

" Have you left your liver behind you ? " asked the jelly fish.

" Yes," said the cunning monkey, " during the daytime I usually leave my liver hanging up on the branch of a tree, as it is very much in the way when I am climbing about from tree to tree. To-day, listening to your interesting conversation, I quite forgot it, and left it behind when I came off with you. If only you had spoken in time I should have remembered it, and should have brought it along with me ! "

The jelly fish was very disappointed when he heard this, for he believed every word the monkey said. The monkey was of no good without a liver. Finally the jelly fish stopped and told the monkey so.

" Well," said the monkey, " that is soon remedied. I am really sorry to think of all your trouble ; but if you will only take me back to the place where you found me, I shall soon be able to get my liver."

The jelly fish did not at all like the idea of going all the way back to the island again; but the monkey assured him that if he would be so kind as to take him back he would get his very best liver, and bring it with him the next time. Thus persuaded, the jelly fish turned his course towards the Monkey Island once more.

No sooner had the jelly fish reached the shore than the sly monkey landed, and getting up into the pine-tree where the jelly fish had first seen him, he cut several capers amongst the branches with joy at being safe home again, and then looking down at the jelly fish said:

" So many thanks for all the trouble you have taken! Please present my compliments to the Dragon King on your return ! "

The jelly fish wondered at this speech and the mocking tone in which it was uttered. Then he asked the monkey if it wasn't his intention to come with him at once after getting his liver.

The monkey replied laughingly that he couldn't afford to lose his liver ; it was too precious.

" But remember your promise ! " pleaded the jelly fish, now very discouraged.

" That promise was false, and anyhow it is now broken ! " answered the monkey. Then he began to jeer at the jelly fish and told him that he had been deceiving him the whole time ; that he had no wish to lose his life, which he certainly would have done had he gone on to the Sea King's Palace to the old doctor waiting for him, instead of persuading the jelly fish to return under false pretences.

"Of course, I won't *give* you my liver, but come and get it if you can!" added the monkey mockingly from the tree.

There was nothing for the jelly fish to do now but to repent of his stupidity, and return to the Dragon King of the Sea and confess his failure, so he started sadly and slowly to swim back. The last thing he heard as he glided away, leaving the island behind him, was the monkey laughing at him.

Meanwhile the Dragon King, the doctor, the chief steward, and all the servants were waiting impatiently for the return of the jelly fish. When they caught sight of him approaching the Palace, they hailed him with delight. They began to thank him profusely for all the trouble he had taken in going to Monkey Island, and then they asked him where the monkey was.

Now the day of reckoning had come for the jelly fish. He quaked all over as he told his story. How he had brought the monkey half-way over the sea, and then had stupidly let out the secret of his commission; how the monkey had deceived him by making him believe that he had left his liver behind him.

The Dragon King's wrath was great, and he at once gave orders that the jelly fish was to be severely punished. The punishment was a horrible one. All the bones were to be drawn out from his living body, and he was to be beaten with sticks.

The poor jelly fish, humiliated and horrified beyond all words, cried out for pardon. But the Dragon King's order had to be obeyed. The servants of the Palace forthwith each brought out a stick and surrounded the jelly fish, and after pulling out his bones they beat him to a flat pulp, and then took him out beyond the Palace gates and threw him into

They beat the Jelly Fish to a flat Pulp.

the water. Here he was left to suffer and repent his foolish chattering, and to grow accustomed to his new state of bonelessness.

From this story it is evident that in former times the jelly fish once had a shell and bones something like a tortoise, but, ever since the Dragon King's sentence was carried out on the ancestor of the jelly fishes, his descendants have all been soft and boneless just as you see them to-day thrown up by the waves high upon the shores of Japan.

The Monkey proposed the exchange of the hard persimmon
seed for the Crab's nice dumpling.

THE QUARREL OF THE MONKEY AND THE CRAB.

LONG, long ago, one bright autumn day in Japan, it happened that a pink-faced monkey and a yellow crab were playing together along the bank of a river. As they were running about, the crab found a rice-dumpling and the monkey a persimmon-seed.

The crab picked up the rice-dumpling and showed it to the monkey, saying :

" Look what a nice thing I have found ! "

Then the monkey held up his persimmon-seed and said :

" I also have found something good ! Look ! "

Now though the monkey is always very fond of persimmon fruit, he had no use for the seed he had just found. The persimmon-seed is as hard and uneatable as a stone. He, therefore, in his greedy nature, felt very envious of the crab's nice dumpling, and he proposed an exchange. The crab naturally did not see why he should give up his prize for a hard stone-like seed, and would not consent to the monkey's proposition.

Then the cunning monkey began to persuade the crab, saying :

" How unwise you are not to think of the future ! Your rice-dumpling can be eaten now, and is certainly much bigger than my seed ; but if you sow this seed in the ground it will soon grow and become a great tree in a few years, and bear an abundance of fine ripe persimmons year after year. If only I could show it to you then with the yellow fruit hanging on its branches! Of course, if you don't believe me I shall sow it myself; though I am sure, later on, you will be very sorry that you did not take my advice."

The simple-minded crab could not resist the monkey's clever persuasion. He at last gave in and consented to the monkey's proposal, and the exchange was made. The greedy monkey soon gobbled up the dumpling, and with great reluctance gave up the persimmon-seed to the crab. He would have liked to keep that too, but he was afraid of making the crab angry and of being pinched by his sharp scissor-like claws. They then separated, the monkey going home to his forest trees and the crab to his stones along the river-side. As soon as the crab reached home he put the persimmon-seed in the ground as the monkey had told him.

In the following spring the crab was delighted to see the shoot of a young tree push its way up through the ground. Each year it grew bigger, till at last it blossomed one spring, and in the following autumn bore some fine large persimmons. Among the broad smooth green leaves the fruit hung like golden balls, and as they ripened they mellowed to a deep orange. It was the little crab's pleasure to go out day by day and sit in the sun and put out his long eyes in the same way as a snail puts out its horn, and watch the persimmons ripening to perfection.

"How delicious they will be to eat!" he said to himself.

At last, one day, he knew the persimmons must be quite ripe and he wanted very much to taste one. He made several attempts to climb the tree, in the vain hope of reaching one of the beautiful persimmons hanging above him ; but he failed each time, for a crab's legs are not made for climbing trees but only for running along the ground and over stones, both of which he can do most cleverly.   In his dilemma he thought of his old playmate the monkey, who, he knew, could climb trees better than anyone else in the world.   He determined to ask the monkey to help him, and set out to find him.

Running crab-fashion up the stony river bank, over the pathways into the shadowy forest, the crab at last found the monkey taking an afternoon nap in his favourite pine-tree, with his tail curled tight around a branch to prevent him from falling off in his dreams.   He was soon wide awake, however, when he heard himself called, and eagerly listening to what the crab told him.   When he heard that the seed which he had long ago exchanged for a rice-dumpling had grown into a tree and was now bearing good fruit, he was delighted, for he at once devised a cunning plan which would give him all the persimmons for himself.

He consented to go with the crab to pick the fruit for him. When they both reached the spot, the monkey was astonished to see what a fine tree had sprung from the seed, and with what a number of ripe persimmons the branches were loaded.

He quickly climbed the tree and began to pluck and eat, as fast as he could, one persimmon after another.   Each time he chose the best and ripest he could find, and went on eating till he could eat no more.   Not one would he give to the poor hungry crab waiting below, and when he had finished there was little but the hard, unripe fruit left.

The Monkey began to pluck and eat as fast as he could.

You can imagine the feelings of the poor crab after waiting patiently, for so long as he had done, for the tree to grow and the fruit to ripen, when he saw the monkey devouring all the good persimmons. He was so disappointed that he ran round and round the tree calling to the monkey to remember his promise. The monkey at first took no notice of the crab's complaints, but at last he picked out the hardest, greenest persimmon he could find and aimed it at the crab's head. The persimmon is as hard as stone when it is unripe. The monkey's missile struck home and the crab was sorely hurt by the blow. Again and again, as fast as he could pick them, the monkey pulled off the hard persimmons and threw them at the defenceless crab till he dropped dead, covered with wounds all over his body. There he lay a pitiful sight at the foot of the tree he had himself planted.

When the wicked monkey saw that he had killed the crab he ran away from the spot as fast as he could, in fear and trembling, like a coward as he was.

Now the crab had a son who had been playing with a friend not far from the spot where this sad work had taken place. On the way home he came across his father dead, in a most dreadful condition—his head was smashed and his shell broken in several places, and around his body lay the unripe persimmons which had done their deadly work. At this dreadful sight the poor young crab sat down and wept.

But when he had wept for some time he told himself that this crying would do no good; it was his duty to avenge his father's murder, and this he determined to do. He looked about for some clue which would lead him to discover the murderer. Looking up at the tree he noticed that the best fruit had gone, and that all around lay bits of peel and numerous seeds strewn on the ground as well as the unripe persimmons which had evidently been thrown at his father. Then he understood that the monkey was the murderer, for he now remembered that his father had once told him the story of the rice-dumpling and the persimmon-seed. The young crab knew that monkeys liked persimmons above all other fruit, and he felt sure that his greed for the coveted fruit had been the cause of the old crab's death. Alas !

He at first thought of going to attack the monkey at once, for he burned with rage. Second thoughts, however, told him that this was useless, for the monkey was an old and cunning animal and would be hard to overcome. He must meet cunning with cunning and ask some of his friends to help him, for he knew that it would be quite out of his power to kill him alone.

The young crab set out at once to call on the mortar, his father's old friend, and told him of all that had happened. He besought the mortar with tears to help him avenge his father's death. The mortar was very sorry when he heard the woeful tale and promised at once to help the young crab punish the monkey to death. He warned him that he must be very careful in what he did, for the monkey was a strong and cunning enemy. The mortar now sent to fetch the bee and the chestnut (also the crab's old friends) to consult them about the matter. In a short time the bee and the chestnut arrived. When they were told all the details of the old crab's death and of the monkey's wickedness and greed, they both gladly consented to help the young crab in his revenge.

After talking for a long time as to the ways and means of carrying out their plans they separated, and Mr. Mortar went home with the young crab to help him bury his poor father.

While all this was taking place the monkey was congratulating himself (as the wicked often do before their punishment comes upon them) on all he had done so neatly. He thought it quite a fine thing that he had robbed his friend of all his ripe persimmons and then that he had killed him. Still, smile as hard as he might, he could not banish altogether the fear of the consequences should his evil deeds be discovered. *If* he were found out (and he told himself that this could not be for he had escaped unseen) the crab's family would be sure to bear him hatred and seek to take revenge on him. So he would not go out, and kept himself at home for several days. He found this kind of life, however, extremely dull, accustomed as he was to the free life of the woods, and at last he said:

"No one knows that it was I who killed the crab! I am sure that the old thing breathed his last before I left him. Dead crabs have no mouths! Who is there to tell that I am the murderer? Since no one knows, what is the use of shutting myself up and brooding over the matter? What is done cannot be undone!"

With this he wandered out into the crab settlement and crept about as slyly as possible near the crab's house and tried to hear the neighbours' gossip round about. He wanted to find out what the crabs were saying about their chief's death, for the old crab had been the chief of the tribe. But he heard nothing and said to himself:

" They are all such fools that they don't know and don't care who murdered their chief ! "

Little did he know in his so-called " monkey's wisdom " that this seeming unconcern was part of the young crab's plan. He purposely pretended not to know who killed his father, and also to believe that he had met his death through his own fault. By this means he could the better keep secret the revenge on the monkey, which he was meditating.

So the monkey returned home from his walk quite content. He told himself he had nothing now to fear.

One fine day, when the monkey was sitting at home, he was surprised by the appearance of a messenger from the young crab. While he was wondering what this might mean, the messenger bowed before him and said :

" I have been sent by my master to inform you that his father died the other day in falling from a persimmon tree while trying to climb the tree after fruit. This, being the seventh day, is the first anniversary after his death, and my master has prepared a little festival in his father's honour, and bids you come to participate in it as you were one of his best friends. My master hopes you will honour his house with your kind visit."

When the monkey heard these words he rejoiced in his inmost heart, for all his fears of being suspected were now at rest. He could not guess that a plot had just been set in motion against him. He pretended to be very surprised at the news of the crab's death, and said :

" I am, indeed, very sorry to hear of your chief's death. We were great friends as you know. I remember that we once exchanged a rice-dumpling for a persimmon-seed.   It grieves me much to think that that seed was in the end the cause of his death.   I accept your kind invitation with many thanks.   I shall be delighted to do honour to my poor old friend!" And he screwed some false tears from his eyes.

The messenger laughed inwardly and thought, "The wicked monkey is now dropping false tears, but within a short time he shall shed real ones."   But aloud he thanked the monkey politely and went home.

When he had gone, the wicked monkey laughed aloud at what he thought was the young crab's innocence, and without the least feeling began to look forward to the feast to be held that day in honour of the dead crab, to which he had been invited.   He changed his dress and set out solemnly to visit the young crab.

He found all the members of the crab's family and his relatives waiting to receive and welcome him.   As soon as the bows of meeting were over they led him to a hall.   Here the young chief mourner came to receive him.   Expressions of condolence and thanks were exchanged between them, and then they all sat down to a luxurious feast and entertained the monkey as the guest of honour.

The feast over, he was next invited to the tea-ceremony room to drink a cup of tea.   When the young crab had conducted the monkey to the tea-room he left him and retired.   Time passed and still he did not return.   At last the monkey became impatient.   He said to himself:

" This tea ceremony is always a very slow affair.   I am tired of waiting so long.   I am very thirsty after drinking so much *saké* at the dinner!"

He then approached the charcoal fireplace and began to pour out some hot water from the kettle boiling there, when

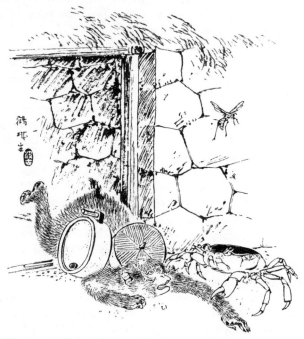

"It was your Father's fault, not Mine," gasped the unrepentant Monkey.

something burst out from the ashes with a great pop and hit the monkey right in the neck. It was the chestnut, one of the crab's friends, who had hidden himself in the fireplace. The monkey, taken by surprise, jumped backward, and then started to run out of the room.

The bee, who was hiding outside the screens, now flew out and stung him on the cheek. The monkey was in great pain, his neck was burnt by the chestnut and his face badly stung by the bee, but he ran on screaming and chattering with rage.

Now the stone mortar had hidden himself with several other stones on the top of the crab's gate, and as the monkey ran underneath, the mortar and all fell down on the top of the monkey's head. Was it possible for the monkey to bear the weight of the mortar falling on him from the top of the gate? He lay crushed and in great pain, quite unable to get up. As he lay there helpless the young crab came up, and, holding his great claw scissors over the monkey, he said:

"Do you now remember that you murdered my father?"

"Then you—are—my—enemy?" gasped the monkey brokenly.

"Of course," said the young crab.

"It—was—your—father's fault—not—mine!" gasped the unrepentant monkey.

"Can you still lie? I will soon put an end to your breath!" and with that he cut off the monkey's head with his pincher claws. Thus the wicked monkey met his well-merited punishment, and the young crab avenged his father's death.

This is the end of the story of the monkey, the crab, and the persimmon-seed.

THE WHITE HARE AND THE CROCODILES.

Long, long ago, when all the animals could talk, there lived in the province of Inaba in Japan, a little white hare. His home was on the island of Oki, and just across the sea was the mainland of Inaba.

Now the hare wanted very much to cross over to Inaba. Day after day he would go out and sit on the shore and look longingly over the water in the direction of Inaba, and day after day he hoped to find some way of getting across.

One day as usual, the hare was standing on the beach, looking towards the mainland across the water, when he saw a great crocodile swimming near the island.

" This is very lucky ! " thought the hare.   " Now I shall be able to get my wish.   I will ask the crocodile to carry me across the sea ! "

But he was doubtful whether the crocodile would consent to do what he asked, so he thought instead of asking a favour he would try to get what he wanted by a trick.

So with a loud voice he called to the crocodile, and said :

" Oh, Mr. Crocodile, isn't it a lovely day ? "

The crocodile, who had come out all by itself that day to enjoy the bright sunshine, was just beginning to feel a bit lonely when the hare's cheerful greeting broke the silence.   The crocodile swam nearer the shore, very pleased to hear someone speak.

" I wonder who it was that spoke to me just now! Was it you, Mr. Hare ?   You must be very lonely all by yourself!"

" Oh, no, I am not at all lonely," said the hare, " but as it was such a fine day I came out here to enjoy myself.   Won't you stop and play with me a little while ? "

The crocodile came out of the sea and sat on the shore, and the two played together for some time.   Then the hare said :

" Mr. Crocodile, you live in the sea and I live on this island, and we do not often meet, so I know very little about you.   Tell me, do you think the number of your company is greater than mine ? "

" Of course, there are more crocodiles than hares," answered the crocodile.   " Can you not see that for yourself? You live on this small island, while I live in the sea, which spreads through all parts of the world, so if I call together all the crocodiles who dwell in the sea you hares will be as nothing compared to us ! "   The crocodile was very conceited.

The hare, who meant to play a trick on the crocodile, said :

" Do you think it possible for you to call up enough crocodiles to form a line from this island across the sea to Inaba ? "

The crocodile thought for a moment, and then answered :

" Of course, it is possible."

" Then do try," said the artful hare, " and I will count the number from here ! "

The crocodile, who was very simple-minded, and who hadn't the least idea that the hare intended to play a trick on him, agreed to do what the hare asked, and said :

" Wait a little while I go back into the sea and call my company together! "

The crocodile plunged into the sea and was gone for some time. The hare, meanwhile, waited patiently on the shore. At last the crocodile appeared, bringing with him a large number of other crocodiles.

" Look, Mr. Hare ! " said the crocodile, " it is nothing for my friends to form a line between here and Inaba. There are enough crocodiles to stretch from here even as far as China or India. Did you ever see so many crocodiles ? "

Then the whole company of crocodiles arranged themselves in the water so as to form a bridge between the island of Oki and the mainland of Inaba. When the hare saw the bridge of crocodiles, he said :

" How splendid ! I did not believe this was possible. Now let me count you all ! To do this, however, with your permission, I must walk over on your backs to the other side, so please be so good as not to move, or else I shall fall into the sea and be drowned ! "

So the hare hopped off the island on to the strange bridge of crocodiles, counting as he jumped from one crocodile's back to the other :

" Please keep quite still, or I shall not be able to count. One, two, three, four, five, six, seven, eight, nine—— "

Thus the cunning hare walked right across to the mainland of Inaba. Not content with getting his wish, he began to jeer at the crocodiles instead of thanking them, and said, as he leapt off the last one's back :

" Oh ! you stupid crocodiles, now I have done with you ! "

And he was just about to run away as fast as he could. But he did not escape so easily, for as soon as the crocodiles understood that this was a trick played upon them by the hare so as to enable him to cross the sea, and that the hare was now laughing at them for their stupidity, they became furiously angry and made up their minds to

Some of the Crocodiles ran after the Hare and caught him.

take revenge. So some of them ran after the hare and caught him. Then they all surrounded the poor little animal and pulled out all his fur. He cried out loudly and entreated them to spare him, but with each tuft of fur they pulled out, they said :

" Serve you right ! "

When the crocodiles had pulled out the last bit of fur, they threw the poor hare on the beach, and all swam away laughing at what they had done.

The hare was now in a pitiful plight, all his beautiful white fur had been pulled out, and his bare little body was quivering with pain and bleeding all over. He could hardly move, and all he could do was to lie on the beach quite helpless and weep over the misfortune that had befallen him. Notwithstanding that it was his own fault that had brought all this misery and suffering upon the white hare of Inaba, anyone seeing the poor little creature could not help feeling sorry for him in his sad condition, for the crocodiles had been very cruel in their revenge.

Just at this time a number of men, who looked like King's sons, happened to pass by, and seeing the hare lying on the beach crying, stopped and asked what was the matter.

The hare lifted up his head from between his paws, and answered them, saying:

" I had a fight with some crocodiles, but I was beaten, and they pulled out all my fur and left me to suffer here—that is why I am crying."

Now one of these young men had a bad and spiteful disposition. But he feigned kindness, and said to the hare:

" I feel very sorry for you. If you will only try it, I know of a remedy which will cure your sore body. Go and bathe yourself in the sea, and then come and sit in the wind. This will make your fur grow again, and you will be just as you were before."

Then all the young men passed on. The hare was very

pleased, thinking that he had found a cure. He went and bathed in the sea and then came out and sat where the wind could blow upon him.

This Man had a kind Heart and looked at the Hare very pityingly.

But as the wind blew and dried him, his skin became drawn and hardened, and the salt increased the pain so much that he rolled on the sand in his agony and cried aloud.

Just then another King's son passed by, carrying a great bag on his back. He saw the hare, and stopped and asked why he was crying so loudly.

But the poor hare, remembering that he had been deceived by one very like the man who now spoke to him, did not answer, but continued to cry.

But this man had a kind heart, and looked at the hare very pityingly, and said :

"You poor thing ! I see that your fur is all pulled out and that your skin is quite bare. Who can have treated you so cruelly ? "

When the hare heard these kind words he felt very grateful to the man, and encouraged by his gentle manner the hare told him all that had befallen him. The little animal hid nothing from his friend, but told him frankly how he had played a trick on the crocodiles and how he had come across the bridge they had made, thinking that he wished to count their number ; how he had jeered at them for their stupidity, and then how the crocodiles had revenged themselves on him. Then he went on to say how he had been deceived by a party of men who looked very like his kind friend ; and the hare ended his long tale of woe by begging the man to give him some medicine that would cure him and make his fur grow again.

When the hare had finished his story, the man was full of pity towards him, and said :

"I am very sorry for all you have suffered, but remember, it was only the consequence of the deceit you practised on the crocodiles."

"I know," answered the sorrowful hare, "but I have

repented and made up my mind never to use deceit again, so I beg you to show me how I may cure my sore body and make the fur grow again."

"Then I will tell you of a good remedy," said the man. "First go and bathe well in that pond over there and try to wash all the salt from your body. Then pick some of those *kaba* flowers that are growing near the edge of the water, spread them on the ground and roll yourself on them. If you do this the pollen will cause your fur to grow again, and you will be quite well in a little while."

The hare was very glad to be told what to do, so kindly. He crawled to the pond pointed out to him, bathed well in it, and then picked the *kaba* flowers growing near the water, and rolled himself on them.

To his amazement, even while he was doing this, he saw his nice white fur growing again, the pain ceased, and he felt just as he had done before all his misfortunes.

The hare was overjoyed at his quick recovery, and went hopping joyfully towards the young man who had so helped him, and kneeling down at his feet, said:

"I cannot express my thanks for all you have done for me! It is my earnest wish to do something for you in return. Please tell me who you are?"

"I am no King's son as you think me. I am a fairy, and my name is Okuni-nushi-no-Mikoto," answered the man, "and those beings who passed here before me are my brothers. They have heard of a beautiful Princess called Yakami who lives in this province of Inaba, and they are on their way to find her and to ask her to marry one of them. But on this expedition I am only an attendant, so I am walking behind them with this great big bag on my back."

When the Princess had looked at the kind Brother's face she went straight up to him.

The hare humbled himself before this great fairy Okuni-nushi-no-Mikoto, whom many in that part of the land worshipped as a god.

" Oh, I did not know that you were Okuni-nushi-no-Mikoto. How kind you have been to me! It is impossible to believe that that unkind fellow who sent me to bathe in the sea is one of your brothers. I am quite sure that the Princess, whom your brothers have gone to seek, will refuse to be the bride of any of them, and will prefer you for your goodness of heart. I am quite sure that you will win her heart without intending to do so, and she will ask to be your bride."

Okuni-nushi-no-Mikoto took no notice of what the hare said, but bidding the little animal good-bye, went on his way quickly and soon overtook his brothers. He found them just entering the Princess's gate.

Just as the hare had said, the Princess could not be persuaded to become the bride of any of the brothers, but when she looked at the kind brother's face she went straight up to him and said :

" To you I give myself," and so they were married.

This is the end of the story. Okuni-nushi-no-Mikoto is worshipped by the people in some parts of Japan, as a god, and the hare has become famous as " The White Hare of Inaba." But what became of the crocodiles nobody knows.

THE STORY OF PRINCE YAMATO TAKE.

THE insignia of the great Japanese Empire is composed of three treasures which have been considered sacred, and guarded with jealous care from time immemorial. These are the *Yatano-no-Kagami* or the Mirror of Yata, the *Yasakami-no-Magatama* or the Jewel of Yasakami, and the *Murakumo-no-Tsurugi* or the Sword of Murakumo.

Of these three treasures of the Empire, the sword of Murakumo, afterwards known as *Kusanagi-no-Tsurugi*, or the grass-cleaving sword, is considered the most precious and most highly to be honoured, for it is the symbol of strength to this nation of warriors and the talisman of invincibility for the Emperor, while he holds it sacred in the shrine of his ancestors.

Nearly two thousand years ago this sword was kept at the shrines of Ite, the temples dedicated to the worship of Amaterasu, the great and beautiful Sun Goddess from whom the Japanese Emperors are said to be descended.

There is a story of knightly adventure and daring which explains why the name of the sword was changed from that of *Murakumo* to *Kusanagi*, which means *grass cleaving*.

Once, many, many years ago, there was born a son to the Emperor Keiko, the twelfth in descent from the great Jimmu, the founder of the Japanese dynasty. This Prince was the second son of the Emperor Keiko, and he was named Yamato.

From his childhood he proved himself to be of remarkable strength, wisdom and courage, and his father noticed with pride that he gave promise of great things, and he loved him even more than he did his elder son.

Now when Prince Yamato had grown to manhood (in the olden days of Japanese history, a boy was considered to have reached man's estate at the early age of sixteen) the realm was much troubled by a band of outlaws whose chiefs were two brothers, Kumaso and Takeru.   These rebels seemed to delight in rebelling against the King, in breaking the laws and defying all authority.

At last King Reiko ordered his younger son Prince Yamato to subdue the brigands and, if possible, to rid the land of their evil lives.   Prince Yamato was only sixteen years of age, he had but reached his manhood according to the law, yet though he was such a youth in years he possessed the dauntless spirit of a warrior of fuller age and knew not what fear was.   Even then there was no man who could rival him for courage and bold deeds, and he received his father's command with great joy.

He at once made ready to start, and great was the stir in the precincts of the Palace as he and his trusty followers gathered together and prepared for the expedition, and polished up their armour and donned it.   Before he left his father's Court he went to pray at the shrines of Ise and to take leave of his aunt the Princess Yamato, for his heart was somewhat heavy at the thought of the dangers he had to face, and he felt that he needed the protection of his ancestress, Amaterasu, the Sun Goddess.   The Princess his aunt came out to give him glad welcome, and congratulated him on being trusted with so great a mission by his father the King. She then gave him one of her gorgeous robes as a keepsake to go with him and to bring him good luck, saying that it would surely be of service to him on this adventure. She then wished him all success in his undertaking and bade him good speed.

The young Prince bowed low before his aunt, and received her gracious gift with much pleasure and many respectful bows.

"I will now set out," said the Prince, and returning to the Palace he put himself at the head of his troops. Thus cheered by his aunt's blessing, he felt ready for all that might befall, and marching through the land he went down to the Southern Island of Kiushiu, the home of the brigands.

Before many days had passed he reached the Southern Island, and then slowly but surely made his way to the headquarters of the chiefs Kumaso and Takeru. He now met with great difficulties, for he found the country exceedingly wild and rough. The mountains were high and steep, the valleys dark and deep, and huge trees and boulders of rock blocked up the road and stopped the progress of his army. It was all but impossible to go on.

Though the Prince was but a youth he had the wisdom of years, and, seeing that it was vain to try and lead his men further, he said to himself:

"To attempt to fight a battle in this impassable country unknown to my men only makes my task harder. We cannot clear the roads and fight as well. It is wiser for me to resort to stratagem and come upon my enemies unawares. In that way I may be able to kill them without much exertion."

So he now bade his army halt by the way. His wife,

the Princess Ototachibana, had accompanied him, and he bade her bring him the robe his aunt the priestess of Ise had given him, and to help him attire himself as a woman. With her help he put on the robe, and let his hair down till it flowed over his shoulders. Ototachibana then brought him her comb, which he put in his black tresses, and then adorned himself with strings of strange jewels just as you see in the picture. When he had finished his unusual toilet, Ototachibana brought him her mirror. He smiled as he gazed at himself—the disguise was so perfect.

He hardly knew himself, so changed was he. All traces of the warrior had disappeared, and in the shining surface only a beautiful lady looked back at him.

Thus completely disguised, he set out for the enemy's camp alone. In the folds of his silk gown, next his strong heart, was hidden a sharp dagger.

The two chiefs Kumaso and Takeru were sitting in their tent, resting in the cool of the evening, when the Prince approached. They were talking of the news which had recently been carried to them, that the King's son had entered their country with a large army determined to exterminate their band. They had both heard of the young warrior's renown, and for the first time in their wicked lives they felt afraid. In a pause in their talk they happened to look up, and saw through the door of the tent a beautiful woman robed in sumptuous garments coming towards them. Like an apparition of loveliness she appeared in the soft twilight. Little did they dream that it was their enemy whose coming they so dreaded who now stood before them in this disguise.

"What a beautiful woman! Where has she come from?" said the astonished Kumaso, forgetting war and council and everything as he looked at the gentle intruder.

He beckoned to the disguised Prince and bade him sit down and serve them with wine. Yamato Take felt his heart swell with a fierce glee for he now knew that his plan would succeed. However, he dissembled cleverly, and putting on a sweet air of shyness he approached the rebel chief with slow steps and eyes glancing like a frightened deer. Charmed to distraction by the girl's loveliness, Kumaso drank cup after cup of wine for the pleasure of seeing her pour it out for him, till at last he was quite overcome with the quantity he had drunk.

This was the moment for which the brave Prince had been waiting. Flinging down the wine jar, he seized the tipsy and astonished Kumaso and quickly stabbed him to death with the dagger which he had secretly carried hidden in his breast.

Takeru, the brigand's brother, was terror-struck as soon as he saw what was happening and tried to escape, but Prince Yamato was too quick for him. Ere he could reach the tent door the Prince was at his heel, his garments were clutched by a hand of iron, and a dagger flashed before his eyes and he lay stabbed to the earth, dying but not yet dead.

"Wait one moment!" gasped the brigand painfully, and he seized the Prince's hand.

Yamato relaxed his hold somewhat and said:

"Why should I pause, thou villain?"

The brigand raised himself fearfully and said:

"Tell me from whence you come, and whom I have the honour of addressing? Hitherto I believed that my dead brother and I were the strongest men in the land, and that there was no one who could overcome us. Alone you have ventured into our stronghold, alone you have attacked and killed us! Surely you are more than mortal?"

Then the young Prince answered with a proud smile: "I am the son of the King and my name is Yamato, and I have been sent by my father as the avenger of evil to bring death to all rebels! No longer shall robbery and murder hold my people in terror!" and he held the dagger dripping red above the rebel's head.

"Ah," gasped the dying man with a great effort, "I have often heard of you. You are indeed a strong man to have so easily overcome us. Allow me to give you a new name. From henceforth you shall be known as Yamato *Take*. Our title I bequeath to you as the bravest man in Yamato."

And with these noble words, Takeru fell back and died.

The Prince having thus successfully put an end to his father's enemies in the West, now prepared to return to the capital. On the way back he passed through the province of Idzumo. Here he met with another outlaw named Idzumo Takeru who he knew had done much harm in the land. He again resorted to stratagem, and feigned friendship with the rebel under an assumed name. Having done this he made a sword of wood and jammed it tightly in the sheath of his own steel sword. This he purposely buckled to his side and wore on every occasion when he expected to meet the third robber Takeru.

He now invited Takeru to the bank of the River Hinokawa,

A Dagger flashed before his Eyes.

and persuaded him to try a swim with him in the cool refreshing waters of the river.

As it was a hot summer's day, the rebel was nothing loth to take a plunge in the river. While his enemy was still swimming down the stream the Prince turned back and landed with all possible haste. Unperceived, he managed to change swords, putting his wooden one in place of the keen steel sword of Takeru.

Knowing nothing of this, the brigand came up to the bank shortly. As soon as he had landed and donned his clothes, the Prince came forward and asked him to cross swords with him to prove his skill, saying:

"Let us two prove which is the better swordsman of the two!"

The robber agreed with delight, feeling certain of victory, for he was famous as a fencer in his province and he did not know who his adversary was. He seized quickly what he thought was his sword and stood on guard to defend himself. Alas! for the rebel, the sword was the wooden one of the young Prince, and in vain Takeru tried to unsheathe it—it was jammed fast, not all his exerted strength could move it. Even if his efforts had been successful the sword would have been of no use to him for it was of wood. Yamato Take saw that his enemy was in his power, and swinging high the sword he had taken from Takeru he brought it down with great might and dexterity and cut off the robber's head.

In this way, sometimes by using his wisdom and sometimes by using his bodily strength, and at other times by resorting to craftiness, which was as much esteemed in those days as it is despised in these, he prevailed against all the King's foes one by one, and brought peace and rest to the land and the people.

When he returned to the capital the King praised him for his brave deeds, and held a feast in the Palace in honour of his safe coming home and presented him with many rare gifts. From this time forth the King loved him more than ever and would not let Yamato Take go from his side, for he said that his son was now as precious to him as one of his arms.

But the Prince was not allowed to live an idle life long. When he was about thirty years old, news was brought that the Ainu race, the aborigines of the islands of Japan, who had been conquered and pushed northwards by the Japanese, had rebelled in the Eastern provinces, and leaving the vicinity which had been allotted to them were causing great trouble in the land. The King decided that it was necessary to send an army to do battle with them and bring them to reason. But who was to lead the men ?

Prince Yamato Take at once offered to go and bring the newly-arisen rebels into subjection. Now as the King loved the Prince dearly, and could not bear to have him go out of his sight even for the length of one day, he was of course very loth to send him on this dangerous expedition. But in the whole army there was no warrior so strong or so brave as the Prince his son, so that His Majesty, unable to do otherwise, reluctantly complied with Yamato's wish.

When the time came for the Prince to start, the King gave him a spear called the Eight-Arms-Length-Spear of the Holly Tree (the handle was probably made from the wood of the holly tree), and ordered him to set out to subjugate the Eastern Barbarians as the Ainu were then called.

The Eight-Arms-Length-Spear of the Holly Tree of those old days, was prized by warriors just as much as the Standard or Banner is valued by a regiment in these modern days, when given by the King to his soldiers on the occasion of setting out for war.

The Prince respectfully and with great reverence received the King's spear, and leaving the capital, marched with his army to the East. On his way he visited first of all the temples of Ise for worship, and his aunt the Princess of Yamato and High Priestess came out to greet him. She it was who had given him her robe which had proved such a boon to him before in helping him to overcome and slay the brigands of the West.

He told her all that had happened to him, and of the great part her keepsake had played in the success of his previous undertaking, and thanked her very heartily. When she heard that he was starting out once again to do battle with his father's enemies, she went into the temple, and reappeared bearing a sword and a beautiful bag which she had made herself, and which was full of flints, which in those times people used instead of matches for making fire. These she presented to him as a parting gift.

The sword was the sword of Murakumo, one of the three sacred treasures which comprise the insignia of the Imperial House of Japan. No more auspicious talisman of luck and success could she have given her nephew, and she bade him use it in the hour of his greatest need.

Yamato Take now bade farewell to his aunt, and once more

placing himself at the head of his men he marched to the farthest East through the province of Owari, and then he reached the province of Suruga. Here the governor welcomed the Prince right heartily, and entertained him royally with many feasts. When these were over, the governor told his guest that his country was famous for its fine deer, and proposed a deer hunt for the Prince's amusement. The Prince was utterly deceived by the cordiality of his host, which was all feigned, and gladly consented to join in the hunt.

The governor then led the Prince to a wild and extensive plain where the grass grew high and in great abundance. Quite ignorant that the governor had laid a trap for him with the desire to compass his death, the Prince began to ride hard and hunt down the deer, when all of a sudden to his amazement he saw flames and smoke bursting out from the bush in front of him. Realising his danger he tried to retreat, but no sooner did he turn his horse in the opposite direction than he saw that even there the prairie was on fire. At the same time the grass on his left and right burst into flames, and these began to spread swiftly towards him on all sides. He looked round for a chance of escape. There was none. He was surrounded by fire.

" This deer hunt was then only a cunning trick of the enemy ! " said the Prince, looking round on the flames and the smoke that crackled and rolled in towards him on every side. " What a fool I was to be lured into this trap like a wild beast ! " and he ground his teeth with rage as he thought of the governor's smiling treachery.

Dangerous as was his situation now, the Prince was not in

the least confounded. In his dire extremity he remembered the gifts his aunt had given him when they parted, and it seemed to him as if she must, with prophetic foresight, have divined this hour of need. He coolly opened the flint-bag that his aunt had given him and set fire to the grass near him. Then drawing the sword of Murakumo from its sheath he set to work to cut down the grass on either side of him with all speed. He determined to die, if that were necessary, fighting for his life and not standing still waiting for death to come to him.

Strange to say the wind began to change and to blow from the opposite direction, and the fiercest portion of the burning bush which had hitherto threatened to come upon him was now blown right away from him, and the Prince, without even a scratch on his body or a single hair burned, lived to tell the tale of his wonderful escape, while the wind rising to a gale overtook the governor, and he was burned to death in the flames he had set alight to kill Yamato Take.

Now the Prince ascribed his escape entirely to the virtue of the sword of Murakumo, and to the protection of Amaterasu, the Sun Goddess of Ise, who controls the wind and all the elements and ensures the safety of all who pray to her in the hour of danger. Lifting the precious sword he raised it above his head many times in token of his great respect, and as he did this he re-named it *Kusanagi-no-Tsurugi* or the Grass-Cleaving Sword, and the place where he set fire to the grass round him and escaped from death in the burning prairie, he called *Yaidzu*. To this day there is a spot along the great Tokaido railway named Yaidzu, which is said to be the very place where this thrilling event took place.

Thus did the brave Prince Yamato Take escape out of the snare laid for him by his enemy. He was full of resource and courage, and finally outwitted and subdued all his foes. Leaving Yaidzu he marched eastward, and came to the shore at Idzu from whence he wished to cross to Kadzusa.

In these dangers and adventures he had been followed by his faithful loving wife the Princess Ototachibana. For his sake she counted the weariness of the long journeys and the dangers of war as nothing, and her love for her warrior husband was so great that she felt well repaid for all her wanderings if she could but hand him his sword when he sallied forth to battle, or minister to his wants when he returned weary to the camp.

But the heart of the Prince was full of war and conquest and he cared little for the faithful Ototachibana. From long exposure in travelling, and from care and grief at her lord's coldness to her, her beauty had faded, and her ivory skin was burnt brown by the sun, and the Prince told her one day that her place was in the Palace behind the screens at home and not with him upon the warpath. But in spite of rebuffs and indifference on her husband's part, Ototachibana could not find it in her heart to leave him. But perhaps it would have been better for her if she had done so, for on the way to Idzu, when they came to Owari, her heart was well nigh broken.

Here dwelt in a Palace shaded by pine-trees and approached by imposing gates, the Princess Miyadzu, beautiful as the cherry blossom in the blushing dawn of a spring morning. Her garments were dainty and bright, and her skin was white as snow, for she had never known what it was to be weary along the path of duty or to walk in the heat of a summer's sun.   And the Prince was ashamed of his sunburnt wife in her travel-stained garments, and bade her remain behind while he went to visit the Princess Miyadzu.   Day after day he spent hours in the gardens and the Palace of his new friend, thinking only of his pleasure, and caring little for his poor wife who remained behind to weep in the tent at the misery which had come into her life.   Yet she was so faithful a wife, and her character so patient, that she never allowed a reproach to escape her lips, or a frown to mar the sweet sadness of her face, and she was ever ready with a smile to welcome her husband back or usher him forth wherever he went.

At last the day came when the Prince Yamato Take must depart for Idzu and cross over the sea to Kadzusa, and he bade his wife follow in his retinue as an attendant while he went to take a ceremonious farewell of the Princess Miyadzu.   She came out to greet him dressed in gorgeous robes, and she seemed more beautiful than ever, and when Yamato Take saw her he forgot his wife, his duty, and everything except the joy of the idle present, and swore that he would return to Owari and marry her when the war was over.   And as he looked up when he had said these words he met the large almond eyes of Ototachibana fixed full upon him in unspeakable sadness and wonder, and he knew that he had done wrong, but he hardened his heart and rode on, caring little for the pain he had caused her.

When they reached the seashore at Idzu his men sought for boats in which to cross the straits to Kadzusa, but it was difficult to find boats enough to allow all the soldiers to embark. Then the Prince stood on the beach, and in the pride of his strength he scoffed and said :

"This is not the sea! This is only a brook! Why do you men want so many boats? I could jump this if I would."

When at last they had all embarked and were fairly on their way across the straits, the sky suddenly clouded and a great storm arose. The waves rose mountains high, the wind howled, the lightning flashed and the thunder rolled, and the boat which held Ototachibana and the Prince and his men was tossed from crest to crest of the rolling waves, till it seemed that every moment must be their last and that they must all be swallowed up in the angry sea. For Rin Jin, the Dragon King of the Sea, had heard Yamato Take jeer, and had raised this terrible storm in anger, to show the scoffing Prince how awful the sea could be though it did but look like a brook.

The terrified crew lowered the sails and looked after the rudder, and worked for their dear lives' sake, but all in vain— the storm only seemed to increase in violence, and all gave themselves up for lost. Then the faithful Ototachibana rose, and forgetting all the grief that her husband had caused her, forgetting even that he had wearied of her, in the one great desire of her love to save him, she determined to sacrifice her life to rescue him from death if it were possible.

While the waves dashed over the ship and the wind whirled round them in fury she stood up and said :

"Surely all this has come because the Prince has angered Rin Jin, the God of the Sea, by his jesting. If so,

I, Ototachibana, will appease the wrath of the Sea God who desires nothing less than my husband's life!"

Then addressing the sea she said:

"I will take the place of His Augustness, Yamato Take. I will now cast myself into your outraged depths, giving my life for his. Therefore hear me and bring him safely to the shore of Kadzusa."

With these words she leaped quickly into the boisterous sea, and the waves soon whirled her away and she was lost to sight. Strange to say, the storm ceased at once, and the sea became as calm and smooth as the matting on which the astonished onlookers were sitting. The gods of the sea were now appeased, and the weather cleared and the sun shone as on a summer's day.

Yamato Take soon reached the opposite shore and landed safely, even as his wife Ototachibana had prayed. His prowess in war was marvellous, and he succeeded after some time in conquering the Eastern Barbarians, the Ainu.

He ascribed his safe landing wholly to the faithfulness of his wife, who had so willingly and lovingly sacrificed herself in the hour of his utmost peril. His heart was softened at the remembrance of her, and he never allowed her to pass from his thoughts even for a moment. Too late had he learned to esteem the goodness of her heart and the greatness of her love for him.

As he was returning on his homeward way he came to the high pass of the Usui Toge, and here he stood and gazed at the wonderful prospect beneath him. The country, from this great elevation, all lay open to his sight, a vast panorama of mountain and plain and forest, with rivers winding like silver ribbons through the land; then far off he saw the distant sea, which shimmered like a luminous mist in the great distance, where Ototachibana had given her life for him, and as he turned towards it he stretched out his arms, and thinking of her love which he had scorned and his faithlessness to her, his heart burst out into a sorrowful and bitter cry:

"Azuma, Azuma, Ya!" (Oh! my wife, my wife!)   And to this day there is a district in Tokio called Azuma, which commemorates the words of Prince Yamato Take, and the place where his faithful wife leapt into the sea to save him is still pointed out.   So, though in life the Princess Ototachibana was unhappy, history keeps her memory green, and the story of her unselfishness and heroic death will never pass away.

Yamato Take had now fulfilled all his father's orders, he had subdued all rebels, and rid the land of all robbers and enemies to the peace, and his renown was great, for in the whole land there was no one who could stand up against him, he was so strong in battle and wise in council.

He was about to return straight for home by the way he had come, when the thought struck him that he would find it more interesting to take another route, so he passed through the province of Owari and came to the province of Omi.

When the Prince reached Omi he found the people in a state of great excitement and fear.   In many houses as he passed along he saw the signs of mourning and heard loud lamentations.   On inquiring the cause of this he was told that a terrible monster had appeared in the mountains, who daily came down from thence and made raids on the villages, devouring whoever he could seize. Many homes had been

A Monster Serpent appeared.

made desolate and the men were afraid to go out to their daily work in the fields, or the women to go to the rivers to wash their rice.

When Yamato Take heard this his wrath was kindled, and he said fiercely :

" From the western end of Kiushiu to the eastern corner of Yezo I have subdued all the King's enemies—there is no one who dares to break the laws or to rebel against the King. It is indeed a matter for wonder that here in this place, so near the capital, a wicked monster has dared to take up its abode and be the terror of the King's subjects. Not long shall it find pleasure in devouring innocent folk. I will start out and kill it at once."

With these words he set out for the Ibuki Mountain, where the monster was said to live. He climbed up a good distance, when all of a sudden, at a winding in the path, a monster serpent appeared before him and stopped the way.

" This must be the monster," said the Prince ; " I do not need my sword for a serpent. I can kill him with my hands."

He thereupon sprang upon the serpent and tried to strangle it to death with his bare arms. It was not long before his pro-digious strength gained the mastery and the serpent lay dead at his feet. Now a sudden darkness came over the mountain and rain began to fall, so that for the gloom and the rain the Prince could hardly see which way to take. In a short time, however, while he was groping his way down the pass, the weather cleared, and our brave hero was able to make his way quickly down the mountain.

When he got back he began to feel ill and to have burning pains in his feet, so he knew that the serpent had poisoned him. So great was his suffering that he could hardly move, much less walk, so he had himself carried to a place in the mountains famous for its hot mineral springs, which rose bubbling out of the earth, and almost boiling from the volcanic fires beneath.

Yamato Take bathed daily in these waters, and gradually he felt his strength come again, and the pains left him, till at last one day he found with great joy that he was quite recovered. He now hastened to the temples of Ise, where you will remember that he prayed before undertaking this long expedition. His aunt, priestess of the shrine, who had blessed him on his setting out, now came to welcome him back. He told her of the many dangers he had encountered and of how marvellously his life had been preserved through all—and she praised his courage and his warrior's prowess, and then putting on her most magnificent robes she returned thanks to their ancestress the Sun Goddess Amaterasu, to whose protection they both ascribed the Prince's wonderful preservation.

Here ends the story of Prince Yamato Take of Japan.

MOMOTARO, OR THE STORY OF THE SON OF A PEACH.

LONG, long ago there lived an old man and an old woman; they were peasants, and had to work hard to earn their daily rice. The old man used to go and cut grass for the farmers around, and while he was gone the old woman, his wife, did the work of the house and worked in their own little rice field.

One day the old man went to the hills as usual to cut grass and the old woman took some clothes to the river to wash.

It was nearly summer, and the country was very beautiful to see in its fresh greenness as the two old people went on their way to work. The grass on the banks of the river looked like emerald velvet, and the pussy willows along the edge of the water were shaking out their soft tassels.

The breezes blew and ruffled the smooth surface of the water into wavelets, and passing on touched the cheeks of the old couple who, for some reason they could not explain, felt very happy that morning.

The old woman at last found a nice spot by the river bank and put her basket down. Then she set to work to wash the clothes; she took them one by one out of the basket and washed them in the river and rubbed them on the stones. The water was as clear as crystal, and she could see the tiny fish swimming to and fro, and the pebbles at the bottom.

As she was busy washing her clothes a great peach came bumping down the stream.   The old woman looked up from

She set to Work to Wash the Clothes.

her work and saw this large peach.   She was sixty years of age, yet in all her life she had never seen such a big peach as this.

"How delicious that peach must be!" she said to herself. "I must certainly get it and take it home to my old man."

She stretched out her arm to try and get it, but it was quite out of her reach.   She looked about for a stick, but there was not one to be seen, and if she went to look for one she would lose the peach.

Stopping a moment to think what she would do, she remembered an old charm-verse. Now she began to clap her hands to keep time to the rolling of the peach down stream, and while she clapped she sang this song:

> "Distant water is bitter,
> The near water is sweet;
> Pass by the distant water
> And come into the sweet."

Strange to say, as soon as she began to repeat this little song the peach began to come nearer and nearer the bank where the old woman was standing, till at last it stopped just in front of her so that she was able to take it up in her hands. The old woman was delighted. She could not go on with her work, so happy and excited was she, so she put all the clothes back in her bamboo basket, and with the basket on her back and the peach in her hand she hurried homewards.

It seemed a very long time to her to wait till her husband returned. The old man at last came back as the sun was setting, with a big bundle of grass on his back—so big that he was almost hidden and she could hardly see him. He seemed very tired and used the scythe for a walking stick, leaning on it as he walked along.

As soon as the old woman saw him she called out:

" O *Jii San!* (old man) I have been waiting for you to come home for such a long time to-day ! "

" What is the matter ? Why are you so impatient ?" asked the old man, wondering at her unusual eagerness. " Has anything happened while I have been away ? "

"Oh, no!" answered the old woman, "nothing has happened, only I have found a nice present for you!"

The Peach split in Two of itself.

"That is good," said the old man.   He then washed his feet in a basin of water and stepped up to the verandah.

The old woman now ran into the little room and brought

out from the cupboard the big peach. It felt even heavier than before. She held it up to him, saying:

"Just look at this! Did you ever see such a large peach in all your life?"

When the old man looked at the peach he was greatly astonished and said:

"This is indeed the largest peach I have ever seen! Wherever did you buy it?"

"I did not buy it," answered the old woman. "I found it in the river where I was washing." And she told him the whole story.

"I am very glad that you have found it. Let us eat it now, for I am hungry," said the O Jii San.

He brought out the kitchen knife, and, placing the peach on a board, was about to cut it when, wonderful to tell, the peach split in two of itself and a clear voice said:

"Wait a bit, old man!" and out stepped a beautiful little child.

The old man and his wife were both so astonished at what they saw that they fell to the ground. The child spoke again:

"Don't be afraid. I am no demon or fairy. I will tell you the truth. Heaven has had compassion on you. Every day and every night you have lamented that you had no child. Your cry has been heard and I am sent to be the son of your old age!"

On hearing this the old man and his wife were very happy. They had cried night and day for sorrow at having no child to help them in their lonely old age, and now that their prayer was answered they were so lost with joy that they did not know where to put their hands or their feet.   First the old man took the child up in his arms, and then the old woman did the same; and they named him *Momotaro*, or *Son of a Peach*, because he had come out of a peach.

The years passed quickly by and the child grew to be fifteen years of age.   He was taller and far stronger than any other boys of his own age, he had a handsome face and a heart full of courage, and he was very wise for his years.   The old couple's pleasure was very great when they looked at him, for he was just what they thought a hero ought to be like.

One day Momotaro came to his foster-father and said solemnly :

"Father, by a strange chance we have become father and son.   Your goodness to me has been higher than the mountain grasses which it was your daily work to cut, and deeper than the river where my mother washes the clothes.   I do not know how to thank you enough."

" Why," answered the old man, " it is a matter of course that a father should bring up his son.   When you are older it will be your turn to take care of us, so after all there will be no profit or loss between us—all will be equal.   Indeed, I am rather surprised that you should thank me in this way ! " and the old man looked bothered.

" I hope you will be patient with me," said Momotaro ; " but before I begin to pay back your goodness to me I have a request to make which I hope you will grant me above everything else."

"I will let you do whatever you wish, for you are quite different to all other boys ! "

" Then let me go away at once ! "

" What do you say ?   Do you wish to leave your old father and mother and go away from your old home ? "

" I will surely come back again, if you let me go now ! "

" Where are you going ? "

" You must think it strange that I want to go away," said Momotaro, " because I have not yet told you my reason. Far away from here to the north-east of Japan there is an island in the sea.   This island is the stronghold of a band of devils.   I have often heard how they invade this land, kill and rob the people, and carry off all they can find.   They are not only very wicked but they are disloyal to our Emperor and disobey his laws.   They are also cannibals, for they kill and eat some of the poor people who are so unfortunate as to fall into their hands.   These devils are very hateful beings.   I must go and conquer them and bring back all the plunder of which they have robbed this land.   It is for this reason that I want to go away for a short time ! "

The old man was much surprised at hearing all this from a mere boy of fifteen.   He thought it best to let the boy go.   He was strong and fearless, and besides all this, the old man knew he was no common child, for he had been sent to them as a gift from Heaven, and he felt quite sure that the devils would be powerless to harm him.

" All you say is very interesting, Momotaro," said the old man.   " I will not hinder you in your determination.   You may go if you wish.   Go to the island as soon as ever you like and destroy the demons and bring peace to the land."

" Thank you, for all your kindness," said Momotaro, who

began to get ready to go that very day. He was full of courage and did not know what fear was.

The old man and woman at once set to work to pound rice in the kitchen mortar to make cakes for Momotaro to take with him on his journey.

At last the cakes were made and Momotaro ready to start on his long journey.

Parting is always sad. So it was now. The eyes of the two old people were filled with tears and their voices trembled as they said :

" Go with all care and speed. We expect you back victorious ! "

Momotaro was very sorry to leave his old parents, (though he knew he was coming back as soon as he could) for he thought of how lonely they would be while he was away. But he said " Good-bye ! " quite bravely.

" I am going now. Take good care of yourselves while I am away. Good-bye ! " And he stepped quickly out of the house. In silence the eyes of Momotaro and his parents met in farewell.

Momotaro now hurried on his way till it was midday. He began to feel hungry, so he opened his bag and took out one of the rice-cakes and sat down under a tree by the side of the road to eat it. While he was thus having his lunch a dog almost as large as a colt came running out from the high grass. He made straight for Momotaro, and showing his teeth, said in a fierce way :

" You are a rude man to pass my field without asking permission first. If you leave me all the cakes you have in your bag you may go ; otherwise I will bite you till I kill you ! "

Momotaro only laughed scornfully :

" What is that you are saying ? Do you know who I am ? I am Momotaro, and I am on my way to subdue the devils in their island stronghold in the north-east of Japan. If you try to stop me on my way there I will cut you in two from the head downwards ! "

The dog's manner at once changed. His tail dropped between his legs, and coming near he bowed so low that his forehead touched the ground.

" What do I hear ? The name of Momotaro ? Are you indeed Momotaro ? I have often heard of your great strength. Not knowing who you were I have behaved in a very stupid way. Will you please pardon my rudeness ? Are you indeed on your way to invade the Island of Devils ? If you will take such a rude fellow with you as one of your followers, I shall be very grateful to you."

" I think I can take you with me if you wish to go," said Momotaro.

" Thank you !" said the dog. " By the way, I am very very hungry. Will you give me one of the cakes you are carrying ? "

" This is the best kind of cake there is in Japan," said Momotaro. " I cannot spare you a whole one ; I will give you half of one."

" Thank you very much," said the dog, taking the piece thrown to him.

Then Momotaro got up and the dog followed. For a long

time they walked over the hills and through the valleys.   As they were going along an animal came down from a tree a little ahead of them.   The creature soon came up to Momotaro and said:

"Good morning, Momotaro!   You are welcome in this part of the country.   Will you allow me to go with you?"

The dog answered jealously:

"Momotaro already has a dog to accompany him.   Of what use is a monkey like you in battle?   We are on our way to fight the devils!   Get away!"

The dog and the monkey began to quarrel and bite, for these two animals always hate each other.

"Now, don't quarrel!" said Momotaro, putting himself between them.   "Wait a moment, dog!"

"It is not at all dignified for you to have such a creature as that following you!" said the dog.

"What do you know about it?" asked Momotaro; and pushing aside the dog, he spoke to the monkey:

"Who are you?"

"I am a monkey living in these hills," replied the monkey. "I heard of your expedition to the Island of Devils, and I have come to go with you.   Nothing will please me more than to follow you!"

"Do you really wish to go to the Island of Devils and fight with me?"

"Yes, sir," replied the monkey.

"I admire your courage," said Momotaro.   "Here is a piece of one of my fine rice-cakes.   Come along!"

So the monkey joined Momotaro.   The dog and the

monkey did not get on well together. They were always snapping at each other as they went along, and always wanting to have a fight. This made Momotaro very cross, and at last he sent the dog on ahead with a flag and put the monkey behind with a sword, and he placed himself between them with a war-fan, which is made of iron.

By-and-bye they came to a large field. Here a bird flew down and alighted on the ground just in front of the little party. It was the most beautiful bird Momotaro had ever seen. On its body were five different robes of feathers and its head was covered with a scarlet cap.

The dog at once ran at the bird and tried to seize and kill it. But the bird struck out its spurs and flew at the dog's tail, and the fight went hard with both.

Momotaro, as he looked on, could not help admiring the bird; it showed so much spirit in the fight. It would certainly make a good fighter.

Momotaro went up to the two combatants, and holding the dog back, said to the bird:

"You rascal! you are hindering my journey. Surrender at once, and I will take you with me. If you don't I will set this dog to bite your head off!"

Then the bird surrendered at once, and begged to be taken into Momotaro's company.

"I do not know what excuse to offer for quarrelling with the dog, your servant, but I did not see you. I am a miserable bird called a pheasant. It is very generous of you to pardon my rudeness and to take me with you. Please allow me to follow you behind the dog and the monkey!"

"I congratulate you on surrendering so soon," said Momotaro, smiling. "Come and join us in our raid on the devils."

"Are you going to take this bird with you also?" asked the dog, interrupting.

"Why do you ask such an unnecessary question? Didn't you hear what I said? I take the bird with me because I wish to!"

"Humph!" said the dog.

Then Momotaro stood and gave this order:

"Now all of you must listen to me. The first thing necessary in an army is harmony. It is a wise saying which says that 'Advantage on earth is better than advantage in Heaven!' Union amongst ourselves is better than any earthly gain. When we are not at peace amongst ourselves it is no easy thing to subdue an enemy. From now, you three, the dog, the monkey and the pheasant, must be friends with one mind. The one who first begins a quarrel will be discharged on the spot!"

All the three promised not to quarrel. The pheasant was now made a member of Momotaro's suite, and received half a cake.

Momotaro's influence was so great that the three became good friends, and hurried onwards with him as their leader.

Hurrying on day after day they at last came out upon the shore of the North-Eastern Sea. There was nothing to be seen as far as the horizon—not a sign of any island. All that broke the stillness was the rolling of the waves upon the shore.

Now, the dog and the monkey and the pheasant had come very bravely all the way through the long valleys and over the hills, but they had never seen the sea before, and for the first time since they set out they were bewildered and gazed at each other in silence. How were they to cross the water and get to the Island of Devils?

Momotaro soon saw that they were daunted by the sight of the sea, and to try them he spoke loudly and roughly:

"Why do you hesitate? Are you afraid of the sea? Oh! what cowards you are! It is impossible to take such weak creatures as you with me to fight the demons. It will be far better for me to go alone. I discharge you all at once!"

The three animals were taken aback at this sharp reproof, and clung to Momotaro's sleeve, begging him not to send them away.

"Please, Momotaro!" said the dog.

"We have come thus far!" said the monkey.

"It is inhuman to leave us here!" said the pheasant.

"We are not at all afraid of the sea," said the monkey again.

"Please do take us with you," said the pheasant.

"Do please," said the dog.

They had now gained a little courage, so Momotaro said:

"Well, then, I will take you with me, but be careful!"

Momotaro now got a small ship, and they all got on board. The wind and weather were fair, and the ship went like an arrow over the sea. It was the first time they had ever been on the water, and so at first the dog, the monkey and the pheasant were frightened at the waves and the rolling of the vessel, but by degrees they grew accustomed to the water and were quite happy again. Every day they paced the deck of their little ship, eagerly looking out for the demons' island.

When they grew tired of this, they told each other stories of all their exploits of which they were proud, and then played games together; and Momotaro found much to amuse him in listening to the three animals and watching their antics, and in this way he forgot that the way was long and that he was tired of the voyage and of doing nothing. He longed to be at work killing the monsters who had done so much harm in his country.

As the wind blew in their favour and they met no storms the ship made a quick voyage, and one day when the sun was shining brightly a sight of land rewarded the four watchers at the bow.

Momotaro knew at once that what they saw was the devils' stronghold. On the top of the precipitous shore, looking out to sea, was a large castle. Now that his enterprise was close at hand, he was deep in thought with his head leaning on his hands, wondering how he should begin the attack. His three followers watched him, waiting for orders. At last he called to the pheasant:

"It is a great advantage for us to have you with us," said Momotaro to the bird, "for you have good wings. Fly at once to the castle and engage the demons to fight. We will follow you."

The pheasant at once obeyed. He flew off from the ship beating the air gladly with his wings. The bird soon reached the island and took up his position on the roof in the middle of the castle, calling out loudly:

"All you devils listen to me! The great Japanese general Momotaro has come to fight you and to take your stronghold from you. If you wish to save your lives surrender at once, and in token of your submission you must break off the horns that grow on your forehead. If you do not surrender at once, but make up your mind to fight, we, the pheasant, the dog and the monkey, will kill you all by biting and tearing you to death!"

The horned demons looking up and only seeing a pheasant, laughed and said:

"A wild pheasant, indeed! It is ridiculous to hear such words from a mean thing like you. Wait till you get a blow from one of our iron bars!"

Very angry, indeed, were the devils. They shook their horns and their shocks of red hair fiercely, and rushed to put on tiger skin trousers to make themselves look more terrible. They then brought out great iron bars and ran to where the pheasant perched over their heads, and tried to knock him down. The pheasant flew to one side to escape the blow, and then attacked the head of first one and then another demon. He flew round and round them, beating the air with his wings so fiercely and ceaselessly, that the devils began to wonder whether they had to fight one or many more birds.

In the meantime, Momotaro had brought his ship to land. As they had approached, he saw that the shore was like a precipice, and that the large castle was surrounded by high walls and large iron gates and was strongly fortified.

Momotaro landed, and with the hope of finding some way of entrance, walked up the path towards the top, followed by the monkey and the dog. They soon came upon two beautiful damsels washing clothes in a stream. Momotaro saw that the clothes were blood-stained, and that as the two maidens washed, the tears were falling fast down their cheeks. He stopped and spoke to them :

" Who are you, and why do you weep ? "

" We are captives of the Demon King. We were carried away from our homes to this island, and though we are the daughters of Daimios (Lords), we are obliged to be his servants, and one day he will kill us "—and the maidens held up the blood-stained clothes—" and eat us, and there is no one to help us ! "

And their tears burst out afresh at this horrible thought.

" I will rescue you," said Momotaro. " Do not weep any more, only show me how I may get into the castle."

Then the two ladies led the way and showed Momotaro a little back door in the lowest part of the castle wall—so small that Momotaro could hardly crawl in.

The pheasant, who was all this time fighting hard, saw Momotaro and his little band rush in at the back.

Momotaro's onslaught was so furious that the devils could not stand against him. At first their foe had been a single bird, the pheasant, but now that Momotaro and the dog and the monkey had arrived they were bewildered, for the four enemies fought like a hundred, so strong were they. Some of the devils fell off the parapet of the castle and were dashed to pieces on the rocks beneath ; others fell into the sea and were drowned ; many were beaten to death by the three animals.

The chief of the devils at last was the only one left. He made up his mind to surrender, for he knew that his enemy was stronger than mortal man.

He came up humbly to Momotaro and threw down his iron

bar, and kneeling down at the victor's feet he broke off the horns on his head in token of submission, for they were the sign of his strength and power.

Momotaro returned triumphantly Home, taking with him the Devil Chief as his Captive.

"I am afraid of you," he said meekly. "I cannot stand against you. I will give you all the treasure hidden in this castle if you will spare my life!"

Momotaro laughed.

" It is not like you, big devil, to beg for mercy, is it ?   I cannot spare your wicked life, however much you beg, for you have killed and tortured many people and robbed our country for many years."

Then Momotaro tied the devil chief up and gave him into the monkey's charge.   Having done this, he went into all the rooms of the castle and set the prisoners free and gathered together all the treasure he found.

The dog and the pheasant carried home the plunder, and thus Momotaro returned triumphantly to his home, taking with him the devil chief as a captive.

The two poor damsels, daughters of Daimios, and others whom the wicked demon had carried off to be his slaves, were taken safely to their own homes and delivered to their parents.

The whole country made a hero of Momotaro on his triumphant return, and rejoiced that the country was now freed from the robber devils who had been a terror of the land for a long time.

The old couple's joy was greater than ever, and the treasure Momotaro had brought home with him enabled them to live in peace and plenty to the end of their days.

THE OGRE OF RASHOMON.

Long, long ago in Kyoto, the people of the city were terrified by accounts of a dreadful ogre, who, it was said, haunted the Gate of Rashomon at twilight and seized whoever passed by. The missing victims were never seen again, so it was whispered that the ogre was a horrible cannibal, who not only killed the unhappy victims but ate them also. Now everybody in the town and neighbourhood was in great fear, and no one durst venture out after sunset near the Gate of Rashomon.

Now at this time there lived in Kyoto a general named Raiko, who had made himself famous for his brave deeds. Some time before this he made the country ring with his name, for he had attacked Oeyama, where a band of ogres lived with their chief, who instead of wine drank the blood of human beings. He had routed them all and cut off the head of the chief monster.

This brave warrior was always followed by a band of faithful knights. In this band there were five knights of great valour. One evening as the five knights sat at a feast quaffing *saké* in their rice bowls and eating all kinds of fish, raw, and stewed, and broiled, and toasting each other's healths and exploits, the first knight, Hōjō, said to the others :

" Have you all heard the rumour that every evening after

sunset there comes an ogre to the Gate of Rashomon, and that he seizes all who pass by ? "

The second knight, Watanabe, answered him, saying :

" Do not talk such nonsense ! All the ogres were killed by our chief Raiko at Oeyama ! It cannot be true, because even if any ogres did escape from that great killing they would not dare to show themselves in this city, for they know that our brave master would at once attack them if he knew that any of them were still alive ! "

" Then do you disbelieve what I say, and think that I am telling you a falsehood ? "

" No, I do not think that you are telling a lie," said Watanabe ; " but you have heard some old woman's story which is not worth believing."

" Then the best plan is to prove what I say, by going there yourself and finding out yourself whether it is true or not," said Hōjō.

Watanabe, the second knight, could not bear the thought that his companion should believe he was afraid, so he answered quickly :

" Of course, I will go at once and find out for myself ! "

So Watanabe at once got ready to go—he buckled on his long sword and put on a coat of armour, and tied on his large helmet. When he was ready to start he said to the others :

" Give me something so that I can prove I have been there ! "

Then one of the men got a roll of writing paper and his box of Indian ink and brushes, and the four comrades wrote their names on a piece of paper.

"I will take this," said Watanabe, "and put it on the Gate
of Rashomon, so to-morrow morning will you all go and look

Watanabe finds the Arm of the Ogre.

at it? I may be able to catch an ogre or two by then!" and
he mounted his horse and rode off gallantly.

It was a very dark night, and there was neither moon nor

star to light Watanabe on his way. To make the darkness
worse a storm came on, the rain fell heavily and the wind
howled like wolves in the mountains. Any ordinary man
would have trembled at the thought of going out of doors,
but Watanabe was a brave warrior and dauntless, and his
honour and word were at stake, so he sped on into the night,
while his companions listened to the sound of his horse's hoofs
dying away in the distance, then shut the sliding shutters close
and gathered round the charcoal fire and wondered what would
happen—and whether their comrade would encounter one of
those horrible *oni*.

At last Watanabe reached the Gate of Rashomon, but peer as
he might through the darkness he could see no sign of an ogre.

" It is just as I thought," said Watanabe to himself; "there
are certainly no ogres here; it is only an old woman's story. I
will stick this paper on the gate so that the others can see
I have been here when they come to-morrow, and then I will
take my way home and laugh at them all."

He fastened the piece of paper, signed by all his four
companions, on the gate, and then turned his horse's head
towards home.

As he did so he became aware that someone was behind
him, and at the same time a voice called out to him to wait.
Then his helmet was seized from the back.

" Who are you ? " said Watanabe fearlessly. He then put
out his hand and groped around to find out who or what it was
that held him by the helmet. As he did so he touched something that felt like an arm—it was covered with hair and as
big round as the trunk of a tree !

Watanabe knew at once that this was the arm of an ogre, so he drew his sword and cut at it fiercely.

There was a loud yell of pain, and then the ogre dashed in front of the warrior.

Watanabe's eyes grew large with wonder, for he saw that the ogre was taller than the great gate, his eyes were flashing like mirrors in the sunlight, and his huge mouth was wide open, and as the monster breathed, flames of fire shot out of his mouth.

The ogre thought to terrify his foe, but Watanabe never flinched. He attacked the ogre with all his strength, and thus they fought face to face for a long time. At last the ogre, finding that he could neither frighten nor beat Watanabe and that he might himself be beaten, took to flight. But Watanabe, determined not to let the monster escape, put spurs to his horse and gave chase.

But though the knight rode very fast the ogre ran faster, and to his disappointment he found himself unable to overtake the monster, who was gradually lost to sight.

Watanabe returned to the gate where the fierce fight had taken place, and got down from his horse. As he did so he stumbled upon something lying on the ground.

Stooping to pick it up he found that it was one of the ogre's huge arms which he must have slashed off in the fight. His joy was great at having secured such a prize, for this was the best of all proofs of his adventure with the ogre. So he took it up carefully and carried it home as a trophy of his victory.

When he got back, he showed the arm to his comrades

who one and all called him the hero of their band and gave him a great feast. His wonderful deed was soon noised abroad in Kyoto, and people from far and near came to see the ogre's arm.

Watanabe now began to grow uneasy as to how he should keep the arm in safety, for he knew that the ogre to whom it belonged was still alive. He felt sure that one day or other, as soon as the ogre got over his scare, he would come to try to get his arm back again. Watanabe therefore had a box made of the strongest wood and banded with iron. In this he placed the arm, and then he sealed down the heavy lid, refusing to open it for anyone. He kept the box in his own room and took charge of it himself, never allowing it out of his sight.

Now one night he heard someone knocking at the porch, asking for admittance.

When the servant went to the door to see who it was, there was only an old woman, very respectable in appearance. On being asked who she was and what was her business, the old woman replied with a smile that she had been nurse to the master of the house when he was a little baby. If the lord of the house were at home she begged to be allowed to see him.

The servant left the old woman at the door and went to tell his master that his old nurse had come to see him. Watanabe thought it strange that she should come at that time of night, but at the thought of his old nurse, who had been like a foster-mother to him and whom he had not seen for a long time, a very tender feeling sprang up for her in his heart. He ordered the servant to show her in.

The old woman was ushered into the room, and after the customary bows and greetings were over, she said:

"Master, the report of your brave fight with the ogre at

Someone was knocking at the Porch, asking for Admittance.

the Gate of Rashomon is so widely known that even your poor old nurse has heard of it.   Is it really true, what everyone says, that you cut off one of the ogre's arms?   If you did, your deed is highly to be praised!"

"I was very disappointed," said Watanabe, "that I was not able take the monster captive, which was what I wished to do, instead of only cutting off an arm!"

"I am very proud to think," answered the old woman, "that my master was so brave as to dare to cut off an ogre's arm. There is nothing that can be compared to your courage. Before I die it is the great wish of my life to see this arm," she added pleadingly.

"No," said Watanabe, "I am sorry, but I cannot grant your request."

"But why?" asked the old woman.

"Because," replied Watanabe, "ogres are very revengeful creatures, and if I open the box there is no telling but that the ogre may suddenly appear and carry off his arm. I have had a box made on purpose with a very strong lid, and in this box I keep the ogre's arm secure; and I never show it to anyone, whatever happens."

"Your precaution is very reasonable," said the old woman. "But I am your old nurse, so surely you will not refuse to show *me* the arm. I have only just heard of your brave act, and not being able to wait till the morning I came at once to ask you to show it to me."

Watanabe was very troubled at the old woman's pleading, but he still persisted in refusing. Then the old woman said:

"Do you suspect me of being a spy sent by the ogre?"

"No, of course I do not suspect you of being the ogre's spy, for you are my old nurse," answered Watanabe.

"Then you cannot surely refuse to show me the arm any longer," entreated the old woman; "for it is the great

In this Way the Ogre escaped with his Arm.

wish of my heart to see for once in my life the arm of an ogre!"

Watanabe could not hold out in his refusal any longer, so he gave in at last, saying:

" Then I will show you the ogre's arm, since you so earnestly wish to see it. Come, follow me ! " and he led the way to his own room, the old woman following.

When they were both in the room Watanabe shut the door carefully, and then going towards a big box which stood in a corner of the room, he took off the heavy lid. He then called to the old woman to come near and look in, for he never took the arm out of the box.

" What is it like ? Let me have a good look at it," said the old nurse, with a joyful face.

She came nearer and nearer, as if she were afraid, till she stood right against the box. Suddenly she plunged her hand into the box and seized the arm, crying with a fearful voice which made the room shake :

" Oh, joy ! I have got my arm back again ! "

And from an old woman she was suddenly transformed into the towering figure of the frightful ogre !

Watanabe sprang back and was unable to move for a moment, so great was his astonishment; but recognising the ogre who had attacked him at the Gate of Rashomon, he determined with his usual courage to put an end to him this time. He seized his sword, drew it out of its sheath in a flash, and tried to cut the ogre down.

So quick was Watanabe that the creature had a narrow escape. But the ogre sprang up to the ceiling, and bursting through the roof, disappeared in the mist and clouds.

In this way the ogre escaped with his arm. The knight gnashed his teeth with disappointment, but that was all he could do. He waited in patience for another opportunity to despatch the ogre. But the latter was afraid of Watanabe's great strength and daring, and never troubled Kyoto again. So once more the people of the city were able to go out without fear even at night time, and the brave deeds of Watanabe have never been forgotten!

HOW AN OLD MAN LOST HIS WEN.

MANY, many years ago there lived a good old man who had a wen like a tennis-ball growing out of his right cheek. This lump was a great disfigurement to the old man, and so annoyed him that for many years he spent all his time and money in trying to get rid of it. He tried everything he could think of. He consulted many doctors far and near, and took all kinds of medicines both internally and externally. But it was all of no use. The lump only grew bigger and bigger till it was nearly as big as his face, and in despair he gave up all hopes of ever losing it, and resigned himself to the thought of having to carry the lump on his face all his life.

One day the firewood gave out in his kitchen, so, as his wife wanted some at once, the old man took his axe and set out for the woods up among the hills not very far from his home. It was a fine day in the early autumn, and the old man enjoyed the fresh air and was in no hurry to get home. So the whole afternoon passed quickly while he was chopping wood, and he had collected a goodly pile to take back to his wife. When the day began to draw to its close, he turned his face homewards.

The old man had not gone far on his way down the mountain pass when the sky clouded and rain began to fall heavily. He looked about for some shelter, but there was not even a charcoal-burner's hut near. At last he espied a large hole in the hollow trunk of a tree. The hole was near the ground, so he crept in easily, and sat down in hopes that he had only been overtaken by a mountain shower, and that the weather would soon clear.

But much to the old man's disappointment, instead of clearing the rain fell more and more heavily, and finally a heavy thunderstorm broke over the mountain. The thunder roared so terrifically, and the heavens seemed to be so ablaze with lightning, that the old man could hardly believe himself to be alive. He thought that he must die of fright. At last, however, the sky cleared, and the whole country was aglow in the rays of the setting sun. The old man's spirits revived when he looked out at the beautiful twilight, and he was about to step out from his strange hiding-place in the hollow tree when the sound of what seemed like the approaching steps of several people caught his ear. He at once thought that his friends had come to look for him, and he was delighted at the idea of having some jolly companions with whom to walk home. But on looking out from the tree, what was his amazement to see, not his friends, but hundreds of demons coming towards the spot. The more he looked, the greater was his astonishment. Some of these demons were as large as giants, others had great big eyes out of all proportion to the rest of their bodies, others again had absurdly long noses, and some had such big mouths that they seemed to open from ear to ear. All had horns growing on their foreheads. The old man was so surprised at what he saw that he lost his balance and fell out of the hollow tree. Fortunately for him the demons did not see him, as the tree was in the background. So he picked himself up and crept back into the tree.

While he was sitting there and wondering impatiently when he would be able to get home, he heard the sounds of gay music, and then some of the demons began to sing.

"What are these creatures doing?" said the old man to himself. "I will look out, it sounds very amusing."

On peeping out, the old man saw that the demon chief himself was actually sitting with his back against the tree in which he had taken refuge, and all the other demons were sitting round, some drinking and some dancing. Food and wine was spread before them on the ground, and the demons were evidently having a great entertainment and enjoying themselves immensely.

It made the old man laugh to see their strange antics.

"How amusing this is!" laughed the old man to himself. "I am now quite old, but I have never seen anything so strange in all my life."

He was so interested and excited in watching all that the demons were doing, that he forgot himself and stepped out of the tree and stood looking on.

The demon chief was just taking a big cup of *saké* and watching one of the demons dancing. In a little while he said with a bored air:

"Your dance is rather monotonous. I am tired of watching it. Isn't there anyone amongst you all who can dance better than this fellow?"

Now the old man had been fond of dancing all his life, and was quite an expert in the art, and he knew that he could do much better than the demon.

"Shall I go and dance before these demons and let them see what a human being can do ? It may be dangerous, for if I don't please them they may kill me ! " said the old fellow to himself.

His fears, however, were soon overcome by his love of dancing. In a few minutes he could restrain himself no longer, and came out before the whole party of demons and began to dance at once. The old man, realising that his life probably depended on whether he pleased these strange creatures or not, exerted his skill and wit to the utmost.

The demons were at first very surprised to see a man so fearlessly taking part in their entertainment, and then their surprise soon gave place to admiration.

"How strange ! " exclaimed the horned chief. " I never saw such a skilful dancer before ! He dances admirably ! "

When the old man had finished his dance, the big demon said :

"Thank you very much for your amusing dance. Now give us the pleasure of drinking a cup of wine with us," and with these words he handed him his largest wine-cup.

The old man thanked him very humbly :

"I did not expect such kindness from your lordship. I fear I have only disturbed your pleasant party by my unskilful dancing."

"No, no," answered the big demon. "You must come often and dance for us. Your skill has given us much pleasure."

The old man thanked him again and promised to do so.

"Then will you come again to-morrow, old man ? " asked the demon.

"Certainly I will ! " answered the old man.

" Then you must leave some pledge of your word with us,'' said the demon.

" Whatever you like,'' said the old man.

" Now what is the best thing he can leave with us as a pledge ? " asked the demon, looking round.

The Demon took the great Lump from the Old Man's Cheek.

Then said one of the demon's attendants kneeling behind the chief :

" The token he leaves with us must be the most important thing to him in his possession. I see the old man has a wen on his right cheek. Now mortal men consider such a wen very fortunate. Let my lord take the lump from the old man's right cheek, and he will surely come to-morrow, if only to get that back.''

" You are very clever," said the demon chief, giving his horns an approving nod. Then he stretched out a hairy arm and claw-like hand, and took the great lump from the old man's right cheek. Strange to say, it came off as easily as a ripe plum from the tree at the demon's touch, and then the merry troop of demons suddenly vanished.

The old man was lost in bewilderment by all that had happened. He hardly knew for some time where he was. When he came to understand what had happened to him, he was delighted to find that the lump on his face, which had for so many years disfigured him, had really been taken away without any pain to himself. He put up his hand to feel if any scar remained, but found that his right cheek was as smooth as his left.

The sun had long set, and the young moon had risen like a silver crescent in the sky. The old man suddenly realised how late it was and began to hurry home. He patted his right cheek all the time, as if to make sure of his good fortune in having lost the wen. He was so happy that he found it impossible to walk quietly—he ran and danced the whole way home.

He found his wife very anxious, wondering what had happened to make him so late. He soon told her all that had passed since he left home that afternoon. She was quite as happy as her husband when he showed her that the ugly lump had disappeared from his face, for in her youth she had prided herself on his good looks, and it had been a daily grief to her to see the horrid growth.

Now next door to this good old couple there lived a wicked

and disagreeable old man. He, too, had for many years
been troubled with the growth of a wen on his left cheek,
and he, too, had tried all manner of things to get rid of
it, but in vain.

The Old Man told his Neighbour all that had happened.

He heard at once, through the servant, of his neighbour's
good luck in losing the lump on his face, so he called that very
evening and asked his friend to tell him everything that
concerned the loss of it. The good old man told his disagreeable neighbour all that had happened to him. He described
the place where he would find the hollow tree in which to hide,

and advised him to be on the spot in the late afternoon towards
the time of sunset.

The old neighbour started out the very next afternoon, and
after hunting about for some time, came to the hollow tree
just as his friend had described. Here he hid himself and
waited for the twilight.

Just as he had been told, the band of demons came at that
hour and held a feast with dance and song. When this had
gone on for some time the chief of the demons looked around
and said :

"It is now time for the old man to come as he promised us.
Why doesn't he come ? "

When the second old man heard these words he ran out of
his hiding-place in the tree and, kneeling down before the *oni*,
said :

"I have been waiting for a long time for you to speak ! "

"Ah, you are the old man of yesterday," said the demon
chief. "Thank you for coming, you must dance for us soon."

The old man now stood up and opened his fan and began
to dance. But he had never learned to dance, and knew
nothing about the necessary gestures and different positions.
He thought that anything would please the demons, so he just
hopped about, waving his arms and stamping his feet,
imitating as well as he could any dancing he had ever seen.

The *oni* were very dissatisfied at this exhibition, and said
amongst themselves :

"How badly he dances to-day ! "

Then to the old man the demon chief said :

"Your performance to-day is quite different from the dance

of yesterday.   We don't wish to see any more of such dancing.
We will give you back the pledge you left with us.   You must
go away at once."

  With these words he took out from a fold of his dress the

There was now a great Wen on the Right Side of his Face as on the Left.

lump which he had taken from the face of the old man who
had danced so well the day before, and threw it at the right
cheek of the old man who stood before him.   The lump
immediately attached itself to his cheek as firmly as if it had
grown there always, and all attempts to pull it off were useless.
The wicked old man, instead of losing the lump on his left

cheek as he had hoped, found to his dismay that he had but added another to his right cheek in his attempt to get rid of the first.

He put up first one hand and then the other to each side of his face to make sure if he were not dreaming a horrible nightmare. No, sure enough there was now a great wen on the right side of his face as on the left. The demons had all disappeared, and there was nothing for him to do but to return home. He was a pitiful sight, for his face, with the two large lumps, one on each side, looked just like a Japanese gourd.

THE STONES OF FIVE COLOURS AND THE EMPRESS JOKWA.

AN OLD CHINESE STORY.

LONG, long ago there lived a great Chinese Empress who succeeded her brother the Emperor Fuki. It was the age of giants, and the Empress Jokwa, for that was her name, was twenty-five feet high, nearly as tall as her brother. She was a wonderful woman, and an able ruler. There is an interesting story of how she mended a part of the broken heavens and one of the terrestrial pillars which upheld the sky, both of which were damaged during a rebellion raised by one of King Fuki's subjects.

The rebel's name was Kokai. He was twenty-six feet high. His body was entirely covered with hair, and his face was as black as iron. He was a wizard and a very terrible character indeed. When the Emperor Fuki died, Kokai was bitten with the ambition to be Emperor of China, but his plan failed, and Jokwa, the dead Emperor's sister, mounted the throne. Kokai was so angry at being thwarted in his desire that he raised a revolt. His first act was to employ the Water Devil, who caused a great flood to rush over the country. This swamped the poor people out of their homes, and when the Empress Jokwa saw the plight of her subjects, and knew it was Kokai's fault, she declared war against him.

Now Jokwa, the Empress, had two young warriors called
Hako and Eiko, and the former she made General of the front
forces.   Hako was delighted that the Empress's choice should

The Empress Jokwa.

fall on him, and he prepared himself for battle.   He took up
the longest lance he could find and mounted a red horse, and
was just about to set out when he heard someone galloping
hard behind him and shouting:

"Hako! Stop! The General of the front forces must be I!"

He looked back and saw Eiko his comrade, riding on a white horse, in the act of unsheathing a large sword to draw

Hako looked back and saw Eiko unsheathing a large Sword.

upon him. Hako's anger was kindled, and as he turned to face his rival he cried:

"Insolent wretch! I have been appointed by the Empress to lead the front forces to battle. Do you dare to stop me?"

"Yes," answered Eiko. "I ought to lead the army. It is you who should follow me."

At this bold reply Hako's anger burst from a spark into a flame.

" Dare you answer me thus ?   Take that," and he lunged at him with his lance.

But Eiko moved quickly aside, and at the same time, raising his sword, he wounded the head of the General's horse. Obliged to dismount, Hako was about to rush at his antagonist, when Eiko, as quick as lightning, tore from his breast the badge of commandership and galloped away.   The action was so quick that Hako stood dazed, not knowing what to do.

The Empress had been a spectator of the scene, and she could not but admire the quickness of the ambitious Eiko, and in order to pacify the rivals she determined to appoint them both to the Generalship of the front army.

So Hako was made commander of the left wing of the front army, and Eiko of the right.   One hundred thousand soldiers followed them and marched to put down the rebel Kokai.

Within a short time the two Generals reached the castle where Kokai had fortified himself.   When aware of their approach, the wizard said :

" I will blow these two poor children away with one breath."   (He little thought how hard he would find the fight.)

With these words Kokai seized an iron rod and mounted a black horse, and rushed forth like an angry tiger to meet his two foes.

As the two young warriors saw him tearing down upon them, they said to each other :   " We must not let him escape alive," and they attacked him from the right and from the left with sword and with lance.   But the all-powerful Kokai was not to be easily beaten—he whirled his iron rod round like a great water-wheel, and for a long time they fought thus, neither side gaining nor losing. At last, to avoid the wizard's iron rod, Hako turned his horse too quickly; the animal's hoofs struck against a large stone, and in a fright the horse reared as straight on end as a screen, throwing his master to the ground.

Thereupon Kokai drew his three-edged sword and was about to kill the prostrate Hako, but before the wizard could work his wicked will the brave Eiko had wheeled his horse in front of Kokai and dared him to try his strength with him, and not to kill a fallen man. But Kokai was tired, and he did not feel inclined to face this fresh and dauntless young soldier, so suddenly wheeling his horse round, he fled from the fray.

Hako, who had been only slightly stunned, had by this time got upon his feet, and he and his comrade rushed after the retreating enemy, the one on foot and the other on horseback.

Kokai, seeing that he was pursued, turned upon his nearest assailant, who was, of course, the mounted Eiko, and drawing forth an arrow from the quiver at his back, fitted it to his bow and drew upon Eiko.

As quick as lightning the wary Eiko avoided the shaft, which only touched his helmet strings, and glancing off, fell harmless against Hako's coat of armour.

The wizard saw that both his enemies remained unscathed. He also knew that there was no time to pull a second arrow before they would be upon him, so to save himself he resorted to magic. He stretched forth his wand, and immediately a great flood arose, and Jokwa's army and her brave young Generals were swept away like a falling of autumn leaves on a stream.

Hako and Eiko found themselves struggling neck deep in water, and looking round they saw the ferocious Kokai making towards them through the water with his iron rod on high. They thought every moment that they would be cut down, but they bravely struck out to swim as far as they could from Kokai's reach. All of a sudden they found themselves in front of what seemed to be an island rising straight out of the water. They looked up, and there stood an old man with hair as white as snow, smiling at them. They cried to him to help them. The old man nodded his head and came down to the edge of the water. As soon as his feet touched the flood it divided, and a good road appeared, to the amazement of the drowning men, who now found themselves safe.

Kokai had by this time reached the island which had risen as if by a miracle out of the water, and seeing his enemies thus saved he was furious. He rushed through the water upon the old man, and it seemed as if he would surely be killed. But the old man appeared not in the least dismayed, and calmly awaited the wizard's onslaught.

As Kokai drew near, the old man laughed aloud merrily, and turning into a large and beautiful white crane, flapped his wings and flew upwards into the heavens.

When Hako and Eiko saw this, they knew that their deliverer was no mere human being—was perhaps a god in disguise—and they hoped later on to find out who the venerable old man was.

In the meantime they had retreated, and it being now the close of day, for the sun was setting, both Kokai and the young warriors gave up the idea of fighting more that day.

That night Hako and Eiko decided that it was useless to fight against the wizard Kokai, for he had supernatural powers, while they were only human.   So they presented themselves before the Empress Jokwa.   After a long consultation, the Empress decided to ask the Fire King, Shikuyu, to help her against the rebel wizard and to lead her army against him.

Now Shikuyu, the Fire King, lived at the South Pole.   It was the only safe place for him to be in, for he burnt up everything around him anywhere else, but it was impossible to burn up ice and snow.   To look at he was a giant, and stood thirty feet high.   His face was just like marble, and his hair and beard long and as white as snow.   His strength was stupendous, and he was master of all fire just as Kokai was of water.

" Surely," thought the Empress, " Shikuyu can conquer Kokai."   So she sent Eiko to the South Pole to beg Shikuyu to take the war against Kokai into his own hands and conquer him once for all.

The Fire King, on hearing the Empress's request, smiled and said :

" That is an easy matter, to be sure !   It was none other than I who came to your rescue when you and your companion were drowning in the flood raised by Kokai ! "

Eiko was surprised at learning this.   He thanked the Fire King for coming to the rescue in their dire need, and then besought him to return with him and lead the war and defeat the wicked Kokai.

Shikuyu did as he was asked, and returned with Eiko to the Empress. She welcomed the Fire King cordially, and at once told him why she had sent for him—to ask him to be the Generalissimo of her army. His reply was very reassuring:

Eiko visits the Fire King.

"Do not have any anxiety. I will certainly kill Kokai."

Shikuyu then placed himself at the head of thirty thousand soldiers, and with Hako and Eiko showing him the way, marched to the enemy's castle. The Fire King knew the secret of Kokai's power, and he now told all the soldiers to gather a certain kind of shrub. This they burned in large quantities, and each soldier was then ordered to fill a bag full of the ashes thus obtained.

Kokai, on the other hand, in his own conceit, thought that Shikuyu was of inferior power to himself, and he murmured angrily :

" Even though you are the Fire King, I can soon extinguish you."

Then he repeated an incantation, and the water-floods rose and welled as high as mountains. Shikuyu, not in the least frightened, ordered his soldiers to scatter the ashes which he had caused them to make. Every man did as he was bid, and such was the power of the plant that they had burned, that as soon as the ashes mingled with the water a stiff mud was formed, and they were all safe from drowning.

Now Kokai the wizard was dismayed when he saw that the Fire King was superior in wisdom to himself, and his anger was so great that he rushed headlong towards the enemy.

Eiko rode to meet him, and the two fought together for some time. They were well matched in a hand-to-hand combat. Hako, who was carefully watching the fray, saw that Eiko began to tire, and fearing that his companion would be killed, he took his place.

But Kokai had tired as well, and feeling himself unable to hold out against Hako, he said artfully :

" You are too magnanimous, thus to fight for your friend and run the risk of being killed. I will not hurt such a good man."

And he pretended to retreat, turning away the head of his horse. His intention was to throw Hako off his guard and then to wheel round and take him by surprise.

But Shikuyu understood the wily wizard, and he spoke at once :

"You are a coward! You cannot deceive me!"

Saying this, the Fire King made a sign to the unwary Hako to attack him. Kokai now turned upon Shikuyu furiously, but he was tired and unable to fight well, and he soon received a wound in his shoulder. He now broke from the fray and tried to escape in earnest.

While the fight between their leaders had been going on the two armies had stood waiting for the issue. Shikuyu now turned and bade Jokwa's soldiers charge the enemy's forces. This they did, and routed them with great slaughter, and the wizard barely escaped with his life.

It was in vain that Kokai called upon the Water Devil to help him, for Shikuyu knew the counter-charm. The wizard found that the battle was against him. Mad with pain, for his wound began to trouble him, and frenzied with disappointment and fear, he dashed his head against the rocks of Mount Shu, and died on the spot.

There was an end of the wicked Kokai, but not of trouble in the Empress Jokwa's Kingdom, as you shall see. The force with which the wizard fell against the rocks was so great that the mountain burst, and fire rushed out from the earth, and one of the pillars upholding the Heavens was broken, so that one corner of the sky dropped till it touched the earth.

Shikuyu, the Fire King, took up the body of the wizard and carried it to the Empress Jokwa, who rejoiced greatly that her enemy was vanquished, and her generals victorious. She showered all manner of gifts and honours upon Shikuyu.

But all this time fire was bursting from the mountain broken by the fall of Kokai. Whole villages were destroyed, rice-fields burnt up, river beds filled with the burning lava, and the homeless people were in great distress. So the Empress left the capital as soon as she had rewarded the victor Shikuyu, and journeyed with all speed to the scene of disaster. She found that both Heaven and earth had sustained damage, and the place was so dark that she had to light her lamp to find out the extent of the havoc that had been wrought.

Having ascertained this, she set to work at repairs. To this end she ordered her subjects to collect stones of five colours—blue, yellow, red, white and black. When she had obtained these, she boiled them with a kind of porcelain in a large cauldron, and the mixture became a beautiful paste, and with this she knew that she could mend the sky. Now all was ready.

Summoning the clouds that were sailing ever so high above her head, she mounted them, and rode heavenwards, carrying in her hands the vase containing the paste made from the stones of five colours. She soon reached the corner of the sky that was broken, and applied the paste and mended it. Having done this, she turned her attention to the broken pillar, and with the legs of a very large tortoise she mended it. When this was finished she mounted the clouds and descended to the earth, hoping to find that all was now right, but to her dismay she found that it was still quite dark. Neither the sun shone by day nor the moon by night.

Greatly perplexed, she at last called a meeting of all the wise men of the Kingdom, and asked their advice as to what she should do in this dilemma.

Two of the wisest said:

"The roads of Heaven have been damaged by the late accident, and the Sun and Moon have been obliged to stay at home. Neither the Sun could make his daily journey nor the Moon her nightly one because of the bad roads. The Sun and

The Ambassadors set out in the Magic Chariots.

Moon do not yet know that your Majesty has mended all that was damaged, so we will go and inform them that since you have repaired them the roads are safe."

The Empress approved of what the wise men suggested, and ordered them to set out on their mission. But this was not easy, for the Palace of the Sun and Moon was many, many hundreds of thousands of miles distant into the East. If they travelled on foot they might never reach the place, they would die of old age on the road. But Jokwa had recourse to magic. She gave her two ambassadors wonderful chariots which could whirl through the air by magic power a thousand miles per minute. They set out in good spirits, riding above the clouds, and after many days they reached the country where the Sun and the Moon were living happily together.

The two ambassadors were granted an interview with their Majesties of Light and asked them why they had for so many days secluded themselves from the Universe? Did they not know that by doing so they plunged the world and all its people into uttermost darkness both day and night?

Replied the Sun and the Moon :

" Surely you know that Mount Shu has suddenly burst forth with fire, and the roads of Heaven have been greatly damaged! I, the Sun, found it impossible to make my daily journey along such rough roads—and certainly the Moon could not issue forth at night! so we both retired into private life for a time."

Then the two wise men bowed themselves to the ground and said :

" Our Empress Jokwa has already repaired the roads with the wonderful stones of five colours, so we beg to assure your Majesties that the roads are just as they were before the eruption took place."

But the Sun and the Moon still hesitated, saying that they had heard that one of the pillars of Heaven had been broken as well, and they feared that, even if the roads had been remade, it would still be dangerous for them to sally forth on their usual journeys.

"You need have no anxiety about the broken pillar," said the two ambassadors. "Our Empress restored it with the legs of a great tortoise, and it is as firm as ever it was."

Then the Sun and Moon appeared satisfied, and they both set out to try the roads. They found that what the Empress's deputies had told them was correct.

After the examination of the heavenly roads, the Sun and Moon again gave light to the earth. All the people rejoiced greatly, and peace and prosperity were secured in China for a long time under the reign of the wise Empress Jokwa.

THE END.

Other TUT BOOKS available:

Please order from your bookstore or write directly to:

CHARLES E. TUTTLE CO., INC.
Suido 1-chome, 2–6, Bunkyo-ku, Tokyo 112

or:

CHARLES E. TUTTLE CO., INC.
Rutland, Vermont 05701 U.S.A.